THE ONLY PIECE OF
FURNITURE
IN THE HOUSE

Also by the author:

NOVELS
Pushing the Bear

SHORT STORIES
Firesticks
Monkey Secret
Trigger Dance

ESSAYS
Claiming Breath
The West Pole

POETRY BOOKS
Boom Town
Coyote's Quodlibet
Iron Woman
Lone Dog's Winter Count
Offering
One Age in a Dream

DRAMA
War Cries

ANTHOLOGIES
*Braided Lives, an Anthology of
    Multicultural American Writing*
*Two Worlds Walking, Writers of
    Mixed Heritages*

THE ONLY PIECE OF
FURNITURE
IN THE HOUSE

A NOVEL   DIANE GLANCY

Moyer Bell

Wakefield, Rhode Island & London

HUMCA

Published by Moyer Bell

First Edition

LIBRARY OF CONGRESS
CATALOGING-IN-PUBLICATION DATA

Glancy, Diane
  The only piece of furniture in the house /
Diane Glancy.

    p. cm.
    I. Title
    PS3557.L294054 1996
    813'.54—dc20   96-8425
                                              CIP

ISBN 1-55921-183-0

"Rachel" is reprinted from *Aspects of Eve*, poems by Linda
Pastan, with the permission of the author and the publisher,
Liveright Publishing Corporation. Copyright © 1970, 1971,
1972, 1973, 1974, 1975 by Linda Pastan.

Printed in the United States of America.
Distributed in North America by Publishers Group West,
P.O. Box 8843, Emeryville, CA 94662, 800-788-3123
(in California 510-658-3453)

We named you
for the sake
of the syllables
and for the small boat
that followed the Pequod,
gathering lost children of the sea.

We named you
for the dark-eyed girl
who waited at the well
while her lover
worked seven years
and again
seven.

We named you
for the small daughters
of the Holocaust
who followed their six-pointed stars
to death
and were all of them
known as
Rachel.

"Rachel"
Linda Pastan

An exile's no honeymoon!

Pelagie-la-Charrette
Antonine Maillet

THE ONLY PIECE OF FURNITURE IN THE HOUSE

Madill, Texas

My father, Wood Hume, worked for the railroad. We followed him from town to town through Texas and Louisiana in the tomato-red sun that sank into the plains. I learned to read on highway signs.

Madill.

Poteau.

Nacogdoches.

The signs rushed toward us for their instant of recognition, then passed into dark.

Runnels.

Waxahachie.

Dead Smith.

Scurry.

Upshur.

Uvalde.

Clegg.

Bethanna hummed and talked to the angels who rushed by like highway signs as we traveled. "With all these children, there wouldn't have been a way." She dried her face with the hem of her calico print. Sometimes an angel would stick to her dress and she'd push it

off. Bethanna could cook and make beds for us anywhere. Other railroad wives came to Bethanna. She
took their children and sometimes they didn't come
back for them. We got Kemp and Wallace, Kileen and
Cumby, that way.

I watched the insects in the headlights as we
traveled.

"How can you tell which ones are the angels?"
Faith asked.

"You just know," Pruddy answered.

"Where is it we steamed like crayfish in the day
and shivered at night?" I asked Bethanna, trying to sort
town from town as we traveled.

"And where is it we're from?" Kileen asked Mamma
as we crowded against her in the truck. I knew she looked
far away in the dark, her eyes still seeing the tomato-red
dusk.

"We aren't from anywhere," Faith said.

"Yes, we are," Bethanna was definite as Cumby's
cough. "We're from Madill, Texas."

And I guess we were as I listened to them in the
dark. We'd lived there more often than not in Bethanna's mamma's house. Wood usually worked in Texas
and then we'd stay in Madill if it were winter and he
went north. We didn't have coats and boots for the cold.
But I would rather stay in Madill with mamma and

grandma anyway, though I was ready to go with Wood whenever he said we'd be moving.

"Madill is where we're going now?" I asked.

"Yes, Rachel," Mamma said with her arm around me and Cumby.

Bethanna's mamma was jolly like Bethanna. They talked through the night when we first got back. I'd wake up sometimes with Kileen and Faith against me and couldn't sleep without the moving of the truck. I'd see the road signs pass and listen to the two women talking in the heat. Then I'd sleep again.

"What's your name?" a soldier asked.

"Rachel Hume." I was at Fort Jether near Madill on Saturday with my sisters Faith and Pruddy. We served coffee and talked to the soldiers. They were like my brothers—Arthur, Mark, Andrew, Kemp, and Wallace.

"Mine's Jim," he said.

I didn't hear his last name. He looked at me and not the others I was with. I didn't like the way he separated me from Faith and Pruddy. I wouldn't talk to him anymore when we went to the Fort on Saturdays.

Bethanna asked me one Sunday after church what was the matter. I told her about the boy as she stirred the bacon and beans cooked with molasses. Jim. I couldn't think of his last name. Bethanna rubbed my back that night in her mamma's house where we stayed in Madill and she prayed with me.

I was quiet those weeks, waiting for Saturdays when I would see Jim again at the army base. But I was also afraid. I would stay with Faith and Pruddy and not talk to him.

"He doesn't do anything, Mamma," I said to Bethanna. "He just looks at me."

Jim was waiting at the curb one afternoon when I came out of school in the fall. He said that he had waited before but missed me somehow. He got out of the jeep and stood in front of me. We were alone like I had wanted all summer, but I didn't know what to say to him.

"Don't you know my name, Rachel Hume?" he asked.

"Jim."

"Jim what?"

"I can't remember."

"Satterethwait."

"That's why I didn't know it."

Bess's marriage dried up, Bethanna told me, because she went too fast. Mamma's words came back to me and I knew why she had warned me.

I thought about Jim in the way the girls told me about when we were in Ashnapper one summer. They brushed their hair back from their foreheads in the woody schoolyard and talked in a hushed manner, looking around now and then to see if anyone was watching them as they searched for words to say again what had already been told. I thought it couldn't be that way but Bethanna said it was.

I wouldn't let Jim take me to Bethanna's mamma's house after school when I talked to him that afternoon. I walked back to the house by myself and sat in the shadow of the plum bushes in the backyard.

On Saturday at Fort Jether, I stayed behind the counter and gave him coffee. He came near me and said my name and asked if he could take me home. I let him take me and Faith and Pruddy to Bethanna's mamma's house afterwards. And Bethanna called him in to meet her and her mother, and grandma stood in the kitchen door and looked at him, and she, who was always jolly, just looked at him.

"Satterethwait," Jim said. "You don't have it yet, Rachel."

"What's the matter with you, Grandma?" I asked when he left. "You're always friendly to everyone."

"I know the enemy when I see him," she said.

"Just because Bess went off with a soldier," Faith said, "you think we'll follow. I can't stand boys myself."

"But look at Rachel," Grandma said.

I flicked an angel off my mouth and went to the plum bushes again and thought of the far places Beth-anna saw as the earth traveled around the tomato-red sun.

Pole Cat Creek, Louisiana

Cumby was sick one night in Louisiana as we went to bed. I hardly had time to think about Jim. In the morning Bethanna was still sitting by the bed, fanning her, though we were into the winter and it was not hot. "Arthur," Mamma called, "find the doctor and your father, if you can."

I could see Arthur through the door of his room. He was in the iron bed with the other boys, except for Andrew, who slept on the floor. Arthur sat up, scratched his head, still groggy from sleep. "Do I haf' to?" he yawned. The reddish light stuck to the wall.

In our room, Cumby's eyes were closed. Her mouth open. She was sweating and her mouth jerked at intervals like she was reading highway signs that rushed past the truck. "She's got fever," Bethanna shook her head. "It's the cough she's always had." Cumby's pale face looked broad. Her damp hair stuck to the sides of her head.

"I'll go find the doctor, Mamma," I said.

"I asked Arthur," Bethanna raised her voice at him. "Arthur!" Soon we heard the door slam.

Cumby turned in bed and groaned. "She's been sick all night," Bethanna said. I'd slept in the same room with her and the other girls and hadn't known. "Rinse these rags in cold water, Rachel, and bring them back."

"Do you want coffee?" I asked.

"Yes, Rachel, after the rags."

Wood came in and went into Cumby's room and the doctor came, also, after a while. Bethanna rested in the kitchen for a moment, stretching her stiff back.

"Wood was down the road in the truck," Arthur told her. "I woke him."

She didn't say anything but returned to the room where Cumby was.

"What's wrong with her?" Arthur asked when Wood came into the kitchen for coffee.

"I don't know. Some sort of fever," he said. The others were still asleep in the four-room rent-house we had in Pole Cat Creek. Wood remained in his chair, staring at the floor.

I folded Bethanna's red apron over a chair beside him. "I could make grits, Wood," I said.

"Has Bethanna got any rice in the pantry?"

"Pudding takes an hour to bake after I cook the rice."

"I'll take grits."

Slowly, the children began to wake. They came

into the kitchen to eat, or they stood at the door of Cumby's room.

"I made a pot of grits," I told them.

"Take the coffee pot into Bethanna and the doctor," I said to Kemp who came in the kitchen and stood by me in a worsted nightshirt with a hole in the sleeve. It had been Arthur's and was faded and worn as the dust in the yard of our rent-house.

"Do you want me to cut the sleeves out of your nightgown?"

"Aren't a nightgown," he grumbled.

"Your shirt?" I said, and he shook his head.

"Is Cumby going to die?"

"I don't think so, Kemp. Take the pot into Bethanna," I said again, but she came into the kitchen with the doctor.

"She wakes in the night talking to herself now and then. She's always had the cough," Bethanna said. "And she feels warm. I thought it was a trace of the swamp fever."

Kemp and Kileen stood by Bethanna, watching the doctor as he talked to her. Kemp had a frown.

Mark and Merrydean fought in the yard. They'd crawled through the window. They were Bess's children. She was my oldest sister. Andrew was her youngest child. I went to the door and called for them to be quiet.

The doctor thought it was swamp fever too. But the possibility of something worse was on his mind. Cumby had nearly starved when Bethanna took her. She'd always been small and slow. The doctor wanted her at the clinic, but Bethanna wouldn't let him take her. Bethanna said it would pass and it would because she believed it. Because outside the angels stood in the yard.

Bethanna saw to a place I'd never been where there was neither sickness nor tears. "We're already there by faith," she said. When I looked through the spaces in her eyes, I almost saw it too.

We went into Cumby's room and stood around her bed. The doctor gave Cumby a shot and she stirred a moment. My arm throbbed where Faith held onto me. I looked down at Cumby's large head and the frail, lumbering body. "Do you want me to call Reverend Houillerie and the church people?" I asked Bethanna.

"No, I think we're enough."

I called the others in. We stood around Cumby and prayed. Wood and Bethanna, Arthur, Faith, Pruddy, Mark, Merrydean, Andrew, Kemp, Wallace, Kileen and myself. "Lord, we lift Cumby to you." We held hands as Bethanna prayed. "She's got something she must have had before we got her. Have mercy. Heal her, Jesus. We look to no one but you."

The morning light slanted from the narrow window, making a pale chute of light into the room on which the angels glided and slid, then ran through the door back outside to slide again. They didn't have wings or even halos, but pushed one another out of the way for a turn. Sometimes one scratched itself or sneezed.

Bethanna continued to pray and we knew Cumby's healing rode into the room on Bethanna's voice. We could hear it thundering from far away. Faith and Pruddy and I were crying when Bethanna finished. Even Wood wiped his eyes.

Sometimes the angels hovered around my tears and I brushed them away.

"We're almost to the top of the hill," Bethanna said.

Mark and Merrydean ran outside while I washed the dishes. That afternoon Cumby's fever broke and the doctor left.

We were in the Cajun town of Pole Cat Creek, Louisiana. Negroes rode on wagons toward the fields. Arthur and Wallace and Mark washed cotton bins. I worked with Bethanna in the house and went to school and played in the pine needles behind our Cajun rent-house. We would be in Louisiana for awhile. Dampness rotted the railroad ties and roadbeds sank. I thought of Jim in Madill, Texas.

But in Pole Cat Creek there were crayfish. We'd sit in flatboats and on the bank of the river. At night we'd cook the fish we caught. We'd sing and laugh and I was under Bethanna's arm. I knew the fire jumping on the faces of those around us, and the darker ones of those back further from the fire, and sometimes Faith and Pruddy and I would sit on the edge of the firelight where it jumped into darkness, until we got cold on the flat, Louisiana bayou, and Bethanna made Cajun bread to eat with the crayfish. "It would be that way with Jesus," she said.

Esmus and Wolfer played the banjo. Burdine sang by herself now. The fire jumped far into the dark after Wood gathered sticks for it again. Faith and Pruddy talked about how to tell the angels from the firelight.

I felt Bethanna's arm. Mamma and Madill and Pole Cat Creek had been everything there was for me. But now I thought about Jim.

Madill, Texas

"Rachel Hume, why don't you tell a person when you leave?" Jim stood before me in town when we'd come back to Madill after the winter in Louisiana. He had on his army fatigues, a hat and a shirt with the sleeves cut out.

My heart was in my throat and I knew the sack of turnips I bought trembled. I felt heat in my cheeks. Everything was wrong. I wanted to get past him.

"What do you mean?" I asked.

"You sure stay on a person's mind," he said. "You could write to me at the base. There's nobody else named Satterethwait."

"Why would I write to you?"

"Because you're trembling and your cheeks are red." He put his finger on my chin.

I pulled back from him, but he took my shoulders to keep me from leaving. "Rachel, wait. I want to see you." He let me go. "Your grandmother isn't friendly. She wouldn't tell me where you were."

"My older sister, Bess, went off with a soldier years ago," I said. "She was fifteen at the time, came back later with three children and died sometime after that."

"Go out with me, Rachel."

I stood before him a moment. "What would we do?"

"Don't you go out with boys?"

"Not very often, Jim. You're too old for me. I don't think Bethanna'd—."

"There's a drive-in."

"I couldn't go there."

"Why?"

"Mamma wouldn't let me."

"Do you have to tell her where you go?"

"Yes."

"The show in town?"

"I can't go to the movies."

"Rachel," he stood before me another moment.

"I have to take the turnips to Grandma."

I said, "Wood comes in on Friday nights, and she makes him turnip stew. It's the only thing she can cook better than Bethanna."

"I'll walk with you."

"No," I said.

"Let me drive you."

"No."

"Rachel, I'm going to be stationed in Germany someday. I thought about you all winter."

"No, Jim."

"Get in the jeep." He took my arm and lifted me

into the seat. He got in and looked at me. "There's no cause to be scared." He started off but he didn't turn down the street where Bethanna's mamma lived.

I held my sack of turnips to my chest and told him that he had not turned where he should have. He took my arm and tried to pull me toward him, but the seats were divided and the floor-shift was between us. He was driving fast and barely missed a car.

We were on the edge of town, and I was almost crying. "Take me home."

But he stopped the jeep at the gate of a cow pasture.

"I want you to go with me, Rachel." He was holding my arms and I struggled away from him. The sack of turnips fell, and I saw his face close to mine. He hurt my arms. I was panicked at the boy I had wanted to be with, had thought about all winter in Louisiana, and now he was closer than I wanted. He put his mouth on mine and I felt the scratch of his face.

I pushed him back with all my strength.

He knew I didn't want to kiss him. Not yet. Wasn't he from a Christian family? I didn't want him to do that. Not yet, anyway. I cried.

He was sorry, he apologized. He just did what he wanted without thinking. He was sorry, he said again. "Rachel." He tried to pull me to him again, trying to calm me. But I cried and would not look at him. He took hold of the door so that I could not get out.

"I can't let you out here, Rachel," he said. "I won't touch you. I won't." But I started to get out again. He grabbed my arm and talked sharply to me. "Stay in the jeep. I'll take you home. I won't bother you again. But you're not getting out. Another soldier would come along." He started the jeep and backed out of the gate with a jump. I picked up the turnips and bumped my head as he started back toward town.

"I didn't know you were like that, Rachel," he said. "I thought you were like other girls. I just thought we'd kiss. I didn't mean to take what hadn't been offered."

He was not what I thought he was. He was not what I had expected. He was rough, coarse, not a Christian boy. I knew that now.

I stifled a sob and the hurt I felt. He was embarrassed as he drove, impatient to have me out of his jeep. I was clumsy as I picked up the last of the turnips.

"Why did you buy turnips when your grandmother's yard is a garden?" he asked angrily for something to say in the awful silence between us as he drove.

"The animals ate them."

"I didn't know nobody had kissed you before, Rachel," he said when we got to Bethanna's mamma's house.

He made me angry when he said that, and I

started to get out of the jeep as soon as he stopped, but he took my arm the same as he had before. "Rachel, I made a mistake. I won't touch you again. Not until you want me to."

I pulled away from him again.

"Sit here a minute. I'm sorry, Rachel. I just thought we'd kiss."

I didn't say anything and he let go of my arm. I got out of the jeep with my sack of turnips and took them into Bethanna's mamma's house to the counter of her kitchen. I went to the backyard and sat in the plum bushes by myself. It had been my place when I was a girl. Now I cried for a boy I wanted and it turned out badly.

"What's the matter, Rachel?" Bethanna asked before supper.

"Nothing, Mamma," I said.

Grandma was fussing at the stove and I didn't want her to hear me. "They wouldn't have got my turnips," she said, "if I hadn't been in bed." Grandma had been sick the past winter. She regretted her illness and the rabbits that got into her yard.

"Jim Satterethwait," I said when Mamma followed me to the back porch where we talked. "He gave me a ride and it didn't turn out like I thought."

"Did he try anything?" Grandma asked when we came back into the kitchen.

"No," Bethanna answered. "Rachel's my virgin. God has her saved for someone."

"Is it always like this?" I asked Bethanna as she put me to bed for the night.

Even the angels listened. I could hear them breathing near my mouth.

"It was for me. But I've only been in love once. I don't know about everyone else."

"Does it last?"

"If you do it right," she said. "I can't wait at times for Wood to come home." It was all right then. If Bethanna talked that way, then it was clean.

Even the angels seemed to go on to other things. Maybe where a dog barked or a neighbor yelled because of whatever happened in the dark outside Bethanna's mamma's house.

I cried that night in my bed for Jim. I remembered the closeness of his face. If he had just waited and not been rough, I would have let him kiss me. I remembered the scratch of his face on mine. It was as though he were still with me.

I felt his presence. It burned in my chest. I had wanted him when I saw him in town, but he didn't wait. Were all men that way? Grandma thought so. Bess would have said so if she hadn't let herself die and were with me now. I turned my face into my pillow and sobbed quiet sobs that hardly shook the bed because

Faith and Kileen were beside me, probably awake, listening to me in the dark, fearing the time they, too, would love.

After awhile I knew the angels came back. Sometimes I could smell them. I saw their sparks in the room. The angels were like small light bulbs that never went out.

Madill, Texas

"Howdy." It was Jim Satterethwait.

Cumby and I had gone to sweep floors in The Old Dime Box in Madill. He stood in the sun and I held my hand to my eyes to look at him. I met him with embarrassment.

"I'm sorry, Rachel," he hesitated.

"You've already apologized. It was my fault. I got in the jeep."

"You had help," he paused.

I started past him but he stood in my way. He took my arm.

"Let go," I said with clenched teeth.

"Are you going to pull away from me again?"

Cumby stood beside me, petrified.

He let me go. "I didn't know you hadn't kissed a boy."

He made me angry.

"Wait," he said. "Now just stand there. It's usually that way with the girls—," he tried to explain. "Usually it's the girls we can't get away from. You just haven't been out enough."

"No, that's not the way it usually is," I said. "Not with the boys I know."

"I don't think you know any boys," he said. "You were scared yesterday in the jeep. No one had gotten that close to you before."

I walked past him and Cumby, who looked puzzled at my conversation with a stranger, quickly followed.

"Go out with me." Jim followed us.

"No," I said angrily.

I saw Jim swat at his face and I guessed the angels were trying to chase him away.

"Just because I was the first one to take advantage of you," he kept saying that. "Is that what you're upset about? Haven't any of your church boys ever—."

Cumby frowned at him and he was quiet.

"That your little sister?"

"Yes," I answered.

"I go to church," he returned quickly, taking my arm again.

"You'll have to if you want to go out with me," I said. "Now don't touch me again."

He let loose of my arm in anger. "I've hardly begun."

I jerked away from him and Cumby and I ran down the street away from him.

"It's a boy that tried to kiss me, Cumby," I explained to her, out of breath when we were walking again to The Old Dime Box. "I liked him once, very much, but now I don't."

I couldn't sleep that night. I crawled in the rolla-way on the back porch in Madill between Wood and Bethanna. He went to the cot on the front porch and I slept under her arm, felt her comfort. No one could hurt me when I was with her.

I cried with my head on Mamma's lap on Saturday night when I thought about Jim. Who was he with? I thought of Jerusha Harwood, whose mother worked at Stojo's.

"It doesn't usually—," Bethanna stopped what she was saying. Wood had gone off to town for the night, probably at Stojo's. Bethanna never went with him because she didn't drink and he needed time with men. "I've prayed for you, Rachel. You're awfully taken with him."

We got on our knees by the bed and I cried. The angels hovered around, fanning us with their wings. Bethanna said that Wood and Grandma were praying too. It didn't seem natural that I had such passion.

I wanted to be with him and felt like I was nothing without him. He was probably with Jerusha, who had all the boys anyway. I cried until I felt sick.

"Pray with me, Rachel," Mamma said.

"He hasn't called me," I said. "I would have said no, but he could have called."

"Grandma doesn't have a phone, Rachel."

The angels had to listen to everything. I knew they plowed my words, hoping my thoughts would come up like a crop of cotton in the field.

On Sunday morning we went to church.

When the sermon was over, I saw Jim at the back of the church. I clung to Bethanna, who talked to everyone.

When we came outside the church, Cumby said, "There's 'er man, Mamma, ther't made Rachel cry." Bethanna saw Jim under the tree and went to talk to him. I looked away, as though I hadn't seen him, and followed Faith and Pruddy who talked with the soldiers. We hadn't been going to the Fort on Saturdays and they asked us to come back.

I was angry with Cumby, who told Bethanna everything she knew.

"You're a lot like her," Jim said at Fort Jether on Saturday.

"Who?"

"Your mamma. The others not so much."

"Bethanna takes in kids," I said. "Some of them are not hers. Three of them are Bess's."

"But you're one of hers."

"Yes. What did she say to you in the churchyard?" I asked.

"She wanted to know if I was saved," Jim said.

"What did you tell her?"

"I said yes."

"You're lying."

He laughed.

"What's the matter?" I asked.

"That's what she said," he answered.

"Do you want coffee?"

He didn't answer.

I poured coffee for another soldier and smiled.

"I want you, Rachel," he said.

Jim upset me with his direct ways. He never varied from that subject.

"Sit with us in church then," I said. "Call for me in the proper way."

"That's not the proper way."

"It is if you want me."

He hit the counter with his hand. "I don't want you in church. I want you to come to the drive-in with me."

"Mamma wouldn't let me."

"Do you have to ask her about everything you do?"

He asked loud enough that Faith and Pruddy and others looked at him.

"Yes," I answered and he walked away.

Jim wasn't in church Sunday morning. I didn't see him that week until Saturday when I went to the base with Faith and Pruddy and several of our friends from school.

"Will you sit in the back with me?" Jim asked.

"Yes," I answered.

But I didn't see him Sunday. I sat with Bethanna and when we were singing, Cumby nudged me. "He's back 'ere, Rachel," she said, "the one ther't made yeu cry."

I turned around and saw Jim on the back row.

"Can I go sit with him, Mamma?" I asked.

"Yes," she answered.

Jim smiled and took my hand. He held it through church. When the sermon was over, Bethanna came back to talk to Jim. I was singing and didn't listen, but I saw him shake his head. Then Reverend Danner asked for those to come forward who would like to receive Christ as their Savior, but Jim didn't move.

On the way back to Bethanna's mamma's after church when Jim had gone, I couldn't speak at first.

"Cumby," I said after awhile, "don't say Jim made me cry anymore."

She looked at me and didn't answer.

"Mamma, he says he's saved but I don't know."

"The Lord wouldn't have sent me to him if he was, Rachel," she said. "Give him time. It's new to him."

"Could we have him to eat with us sometime?"

"Yes," she said.

I didn't see Jim for another week. He didn't come to church on Sunday morning, and I hadn't gone to Fort Jether the day before because I had to can with Bethanna and Grandma. I had seen an army jeep parked at the curb one afternoon when I left school, but they looked alike and I couldn't tell if it were Jim's or not.

But one evening Cumby hurried in looking flushed. "Rachel, ther man's across th' road ther't want t' talk t' yeu. Are yeu goin', Rachel?"

She looked at me anxiously.

"Yes," I answered. "It's all right, Cumby."

"If you want to talk to me," I called to Jim, "you can come on the porch."

"I want to talk to you, Rachel," Jim said at the gate, "but I'm not coming on the porch."

"The light's burnt out."

"We'll talk here. You don't have a phone. You didn't come to the base Saturday."

"I had—," I started to say.

"You won't go anywhere with me," he interrupted. Some of my brothers and sisters were on the porch-swing and I knew they listened. We stood a moment before each other and I felt that same bond to him. I knew that my cheeks were red and I was trembling. He took my shoulders with his hand and I didn't pull back. He kissed me with his arms around me until I thought my breath would leave.

"You're clean, Rachel. I can't go the places I used to. I'll come to church with you." He still had his arms around me.

"Let's walk down the road," I said.

He held my hand as we walked together.

"When are your folks leaving again?"

"I don't know," I told him. "Wood just comes in and says we're going." I loved Mamma and God and now I wanted Jim as much as I did them. "I hope we don't leave Madill," I said, "ever—."

We turned around and walked back toward Beth-anna's mamma's house.

"When are you going to Germany?" I asked.

"It's coming," he said.

He let my hand go when we got to the gate and I stood by him a moment. "I have to go back to the base."

He kissed me again, and I ran up the steps of Bethanna'a mamma's house where the kids sat on the porch.

"Swing with us," Wallace said.

"Leave me alone for awhile," I answered.

"Go out with me," Jim said when I went to Fort Jether on Saturday with Faith and Pruddy.

Kileen had taken my place at The Old Dime Box with Cumby because I had to tell Jim that we were leaving Madill.

"I'll ask Bethanna if I can."

"Rachel," he hesitated a moment. "You're old enough to go without asking."

"Bethanna wants us to ask her."

"How do you know? You never go anywhere with anyone."

Jim was hurting me again. I had cried before I came to the base because I had to tell him Wood said we'd be moving back to Louisiana.

"Do we have to?" I had asked.

"Yes," Bethanna had answered, "all of us."

I wanted to tell Jim that we were leaving Madill, but I could see that he was impatient with me.

"If I didn't have Bethanna," I told him bluntly, "I would let you have me, Jim, and I would have a baby like Bess did. I want to finish school. It isn't time."

"I'm not asking you to have a baby, Rachel. I just want to go out with you."

"Come to church tomorrow. I'll sit with you."

He stood at the counter a moment. "No."

I knew he was angry. "You said you would."

"I've changed my mind, Rachel," he said. "I follow enough orders from the army."

Jim Satterethwait came up the road in his jeep Sunday morning as we were leaving for church. "Got room for one more?" he asked Wood.

Bethanna and Bethanna's mamma were in the truck with Wood. I could hear her hum. Wood turned around where all of us were behind him in the truck. "If you can find a place," he said.

"You wouldn't want to ride with me, would you, Rachel?"

"No," I said.

"I'll ride—," Arthur said but Jim ignored him.

"Rachel, we want to ride in the jeep," Wallace explained. Kemp frowned at me.

Jim parked the jeep and climbed in the truck beside me. The others greeted him—Mark, Merrydean, Andrew, then Arthur, Kemp, Wallace, Faith, Pruddy, Kileen. Even the angels. Jim wanted to hold

Cumby on his lap, but she moved over on Arthur's lap to make room for him.

Jim looked at me. "Just like you," he said.

We would be leaving Madill and I hadn't told Jim yet. As we sat among my brothers and sisters, I thought I would leave without telling Jim. It would be easier. But after dinner when Jim had left for maneuvers, Bethanna said I should tell him.

"I couldn't do it without you, Mamma," I said after we talked.

"It's for the best," Grandma said from the other room, "though you may not see it now."

"I have Bess to remember," I said.

Pole Cat Creek, Louisiana

Before two weeks had passed, we moved back to Pole Cat Creek. Wood stayed with us on the porch when I told Jim.

Mamma was sick by the time we found a rent-house. She went to bed while we moved into the un-painted place.

"Keep the children away from the creek," she said as we put the cardboard suitcase for our clothes under the bed. "Bless the Lord."

"Don't talk like that, Mamma. It sounds like you're dying," Pruddy told her.

I hated those times Bethanna was sick. None of us could get along without her. Even the angels seemed to move like earthworms across the floor. Cumby's fever also returned. They stayed in bed together and we prayed for them both when Reverend Houillerie came to the house. Cumby changed as she got older. Her forehead broadened and she was slower. "She isn't go-ing to be attractive," Bethanna's mamma had said.

"Pole Cat Creek is where we are cold at night and hot in the day," I said to Bethanna one evening as I sat on the edge of her bed. "But it's late in the fall before winter comes."

"The dampness hangs on at night," she said. "I think I'll be able to get up soon, Rachel. I hear the angels stirring in the room. I feel them pulling at my feet."

The men played cards on the back porch in Pole Cat Creek and Mamma Bethanna got up and boiled shrimp for them in the backyard one night. Wood lost his cards to Virgil for watching Mamma.

Roy was there, talking about a woman in town. I knew who she was. Arthur had pointed her out to me. Wolfer and Virgil were going to try her.

"Hush," Mamma told them. "There's children in the yard."

They'd just go to town then and play cards, Roy said. "Or else the women and children could just stay in the house."

But Wood settled Roy.

Bethanna boiled more shrimp and the men ate and drank beer while they played cards and we ate in the kitchen because Mamma wouldn't let us eat in the yard although Arthur heard every word they said and Mark had already climbed out the back-screen window.

Wood traveled from Louisiana to Kansas and Oklahoma that winter for the railroad. We didn't return to Madill because Bethanna didn't have the strength.

"You might not be here to harvest them," Wood said when he was back in Louisiana and Bethanna planted tomatoes by the rent-house in Pole Cat Creek in the spring. "We might be moving again."

"I know," she said. "But somone'll be here to eat them."

I saw Faith in the garden with her hair wrapped in a red-print scarf. The morning sun lit the cambric sleeves of the blouse she wore as she bent over the rows and weeded. She was the prettiest of us, I thought.

I wrote Jim a letter after I hoed for Bethanna. Sometimes we sent him Bible scriptures. "He might as well know who you are and what you stand for," Bethanna said. "There isn't a life without Jesus, Rachel."

"Will I ever see him again, Mamma?"

"If you're the one God has for him, Rachel. I don't know yet. He isn't a Christian. You can't marry an unbeliever."

"He will be a Christian, Mamma."

"I thought God had someone other than Jim for you."

"Do you think so?"

"You're still young."

"I'm older than you were when you married Wood Hume."

"It was different then."

"How was it different, mamma?"

"You are going to finish school, have something you can do. If you kept books at The Old Dime Box, did something like that, you wouldn't have such a hard time with money. It killed Bess, not having anything."

"Jim said I was like you, Mamma."

She laughed. "I like him though," she admitted.

I think the angels kicked their feet at one another as we talked. I could hear their toenails click.

Madill, Texas

Bethanna's mamma died suddenly early in the summer. We had no warning. It looked as though she just didn't wake up one morning.

Reverend Danner in Madill called Reverend Houillerie in Pole Cat Creek because we never had a phone.

We returned to Madill on the train. Jim met us at the station. "The Lord be praised," Bethanna said as she wiped her tears with the hem of her poplin dress.

Jim Satterethwait was in his dress uniform. Wood, Mamma Bethanna, and the younger children got in his jeep. He took them to Grandma's house, then returned shortly for the rest of us.

"Guess I'll have to get used to your sudden moves," Jim said.

I sat on the edge of his seat with him. I could have sat by Arthur, but I wanted to be by Jim. Faith, Pruddy and Mark were in the backseat with the suitcase.

"Wait before you go in the house," Jim said at the gate.

"Bethanna needs me," I told him. "She's grieving over Grandma."

"I need you too," Jim said. "Just wait a minute. I'm going to Germany in two months."

I was startled. "For how long?"

"A year," he said and held me as I stood on the porch. A few people came to call on Bethanna and they looked at us as they passed.

"Rachel, I've got to get back to the base but I want to tell you something."

"What?"

"There was a poker game I was going to one night. A fellow got stabbed and I would have been in the middle of it. But your letter came and I decided not to go. I wouldn't have been promoted—."

"Mamma prays for you."

He kissed me and dried my tears with his handkerchief. "Do you?"

"Yes, Jim."

We sat in the front pews of the Madill Grace Church. The choir of four was before us and I listened to them sing:

> I'll fly away / O Lordy
> I'll fly away.

"I'll rune der 'ay," Cumby sang off tune with them. She also clapped her hands off beat.

> When I'm gone /
> Hallelujah / by and by /
> I'll fly away.

"Er'll goin' 'ay," Cumby finished.

Beth Howry's coffin was before us at the altar of the church. How strange her name looked on the card I held in my hand. Her straw garden hat had plum blossoms on it. Her sister, Maclyn Howry, a fidgety woman in an old straw hat, sat beside Jim and me.

Reverend Danner said that the grave has lost its sting and though we sorrow, we are not like others who have no hope.

"She's talking to Bess," Mamma Bethanna leaned to me.

"Do you think so, Mamma?"

"Yes. And she's praising Jesus. It's not what we see that matters, Rachel," she said when we were still on the front pews after the funeral, "but what we don't see. It's the way of faith. What else are we here for, but to prepare to be with Him?"

I saw them take the old garden hat with plum blossoms from the coffin. They gave it to Bethanna and we followed the men from the church—Wood, Arthur, Mark, a Howry from the West Texas plains, a neighbor, and an elder. Bethanna's mamma would be buried in the cemetery south of Madill.

"Be grateful she didn't linger," they comforted Bethanna under the pine trees by the grave. "She could have suffered like my mother," a woman told Mamma, "out of her mind, shriveled, don't know anybody. Yet she lives. Can't understand it. Be thankful, Sister Bethanna," the woman said in tears and moved on.

Others passed before us at Grandma's grave in the cemetery, comforting Bethanna, all the while wiping their eyes, grieving as though from their own buried sorrows.

Some passed with strange eyes. I didn't know them. Lydia. Ebulus. Or Dorcus. Those names came to mind. Maybe they were saints, those believers from the Old and New Testaments, returned now and then to help us with our faith. Not always there like the angels.

After the funeral, we couldn't find Mark. Jim looked in Madill for him.

"Were you at Stojo's?" I asked.

"I stopped there for him," Jim said, "but Jerusha hadn't seen him."

I stiffened when I knew he talked to Jerusha Harwood.

Bethanna grieved also for Mark. She knew he was gone. He was her first grandchild—almost as old as Arthur, Faith and I, because she had Bess long before the rest of us were born. She wept at the table in Grandma's house that Wood had made. It was almost as long as the room.

In two days, we were to leave Madill. Wood had to return to work, and she didn't like for the family to be separated. But the will had not been read, and she would have to make another trip from Louisiana if she didn't stay until the lawyer returned from Arkansas.

Bethanna wanted me to go back to Pole Cat Creek with Wood and the children but I wanted to stay in Madill with her and Jim.

"Faith can cook. Send her, Mamma, with them."

Wood, Arthur, Faith, Pruddy, Wallace, Merry-dean, and Andrew returned to Pole Cat Creek because most of them had school and jobs in the cotton fields. I stayed in Madill with Bethanna and the two younger children. Kemp and Cumby were on the front steps of Grandma's house when Jim drove up in his jeep. They called to me.

"I got the night off. Go out with me, Rachel," Jim said. "We've never really been on a date."

"Where would we go?"

"To the movies," he said.

Cumby turned sharply to me. Bethanna wouldn't let us go to the movies. She'd been through that already with Faith and Pruddy, even Merrydean.

"Maybe Cumby would like to come," Jim smiled.

She shook her head that she would not.

"Come for a ride with me, Rachel, just for awhile."

"I'll ask Bethanna."

Jim looked at the ceiling of the porch. It still exasperated him that I had to ask Bethanna. Cumby thought she could come with us, if it were just for a ride.

"I'll take you sometime, Cumby," he answered, "but now I want to be with Rachel by myself."

I drove off with Jim, leaving Cumby and Kemp on the front step.

Jim drove to the pasture gate where we'd been the first time I was in his jeep. He kissed me several times. "I love you, Rachel," he said. "I want you so."

"I've been with Bethanna too long," I pulled away from him. "I can't until I'm married."

"Married?" he said. "Do I have to wait that long?"

"If it's me you marry," I said. "It's God's truth, Jim. We would be sorry later. I would be sorry later. I saw it happen to Bess."

"Because it happened to Bess. Do you think that happens to everyone just because it happened to Bess? I'm tired of hearing about Bess. That's all you talk about when we're together. I want *you*, Rachel," he said again, taking ahold of me.

I knew he ached for me, and I would have given myself if it weren't for God and Bethanna and the angels who sat on my lap. I loved Bethanna all the more for the strength she had given me. She knew the temptation I would have.

"I love you, Jim, and would do anything for you, but not that."

"You'll drive me to Jerusha," he hit the steering wheel with his hands, started the jeep, and backed from the pasture gate with a jerk, just as he had when I gathered the sack of spilled turnips.

"I'm going to be a pillar like Bethanna," I cried as he started down the road toward Madill. "I couldn't be anything else. She raised me. You don't understand."

"No, I don't." He shook his head.

"Come with us to the revival. Reverend Danner is holding meetings this week. There is no hope for us unless you are a Christian also."

"I am a Christian." He turned the corner sharply into Madill. "You're always trying to get me to the altar," he said impatiently.

I didn't say anything else.

"You are a hard woman, Rachel," he said when we came to Bethanna's mamma's house.

"On the contrary—," I said and started to get out of the jeep.

"Times have changed." He held my arm. "Bethanna is left over from the Civil War—and you with her, Miss Hume. People's ideas have changed—."

"But God's haven't." I felt a strange power over

Jim because I had refused to do what I knew shouldn't be done.

"You could go to Germany with me."

I looked at him.

"As my wife," he finished.

"You know what Bethanna would say."

"It's not her that I'm asking."

"But I wouldn't go without her permission."

"Does it ever bother you, Rachel—," he paused.

"Yes," I answered, "but not as much as the guilt would." I got out of Jim's jeep and went into the house. I knew he was angry. I no longer felt any power over him. Only hurt. I loved him and wanted him, and he might be going to Jerusha. I would be forgiven by Bethanna and God, but it wouldn't have been the same as if I had waited. Jerusha could have him. I slammed the door.

"She could have lingered, Rachel, and I would have been torn between her and Wood and the children." Bethanna had been sitting in the house alone when I got back. Kemp and Cumby were in bed. "I should have been with her." Bethanna saddened me. "But God took her, Rachel; he never gives us more than we can carry. He knew I had enough with Mark and the children. He'll never let you down, Rachel, remember that." I sat at her feet with my head in her lap. We cried together in the small house that was dark but for a lamp in the other room and the light of the angels. We were in the kitchen at the long table with enough chairs, Jim had said, to seat the army.

I sat against Bethanna for a long time and sobbed when I thought of him.

Reverend Danner delivered his revival sermon in the Madill Grace Church. Jim sat beside me, and I knew he raised his hand when Reverend Danner asked for those who wanted to be saved. But at the invitation to come forward to the altar, Jim stayed in his seat. Bethanna talked to him but he didn't move.

I went to the altar. Others had come, praying silently. Several came to be saved and Reverend Danner was speaking to them. I prayed for Jim's salvation. Tears ran down my cheeks. It was nearly time for us to go back to Pole Cat Creek. I couldn't stand for him not to be saved. Then I knew he was at the altar with Bethanna. She had her Bible and was showing him scripture. She read from Isaiah that we have turned to our own way. But Jesus bore our griefs and sorrows. He was wounded for our transgressions and by his stripes we are healed.

"Have you asked Jesus to be your Savior?" Reverend Danner repeated.

Jim shook his head that he hadn't.

"Would you accept Jesus as your Savior?"

Jim paused.

"Otherwise you are lost in your sins before God."

"Would you like to accept God's way of salvation?" Bethanna asked him.

"I don't understand it," Jim said, "but I'll accept it."

"God chose a way that would be hard to understand," Reverend Danner spoke to Jim. "There's no man righteous," he told him. "God has given his Son for the cleansing of our sins, that whoever believes in Him should have everlasting life."

Jim looked down as the angels leaped across the floor. Some leaned against him, wiping his forehead. I stepped on one of their toes by mistake and heard it squeal.

"Where is Jesus now?" Reverend Danner asked.

"I don't know," Jim answered.

"I am always with you, even to the end of the world. That's Matthew twenty-eight and twenty," Reverend Danner read.

Jim bowed his head at the altar and cried with great sobs for a moment. When he finished he looked up embarrassed. I kissed him at the altar of the Madill Grace Church.

"I have never cared for you more," I told him.

"Jim is away from his family." Bethanna and I were going through Grandma's kitchen—her earthenware and tin plates, the apple baker and jelly molds, her hen tureen, the cast-iron pots.

"He needs me, Bethanna. I was thinking that I would stay in Madill and finish school and be with Jim. He's going to Germany in two months. I could even go with him and finish school later."

"I knew it was coming, Rachel. No."

"I could work at The Dime Box—."

"No, Rachel. It's too soon. You aren't through with school. You aren't ready to marry. It's a blessing that Jim's going to Germany for a year. It's just the time you need. You aren't ready to be a wife."

"But he's leaving, Ma—."

"No, Rachel. Give him up for awhile. He will return if he is the man God has for you."

"Mamma—."

"Don't bother me now, Rachel. I'm grieved over my mamma and worried about Mark. You don't even realize that we haven't heard from him. When we get Grandma's things settled, we're returning to Louisiana."

I ran from the house into the plum bushes and sobbed to myself. When I looked up, Kemp and Cumby were watching me with a frown.

"How old are you, Mamma?" I was back in the house.

"Forty-five."

"How old were you when you had Bess?"

"Fifteen. But it was eight years before I had Arthur and even later for you."

"And Bess was how old when she had Mark?"

"Sixteen."

"My age, Mamma, and you won't let me stay in Madill. Grandma's house is here—."

"Rachel, you are going back to Pole Cat Creek with me."

I stomped out to the front porch. I surmised by the shadow of the tree across the road that it was about four o'clock. He could have been here by now.

I waited for Jim on the porch, but Mamma came out. "I've spoiled you, Rachel. You get nearly everything you want. But Jim is a different matter. It's for the rest of your life. When you enter into a marriage, you make a stable place to raise a family. Otherwise, your hopes turn to bitterness and you get up each day with children and worry and debt and trouble."

I understood what she said.

"Do you want any of Grandma's belongings?"

"The lace off her other Sunday dress," I said, "for my wedding dress, and I want my wedding now."

"You're eager for responsibility, Rachel," Bethanna said. "I think I'll leave everything here. We'll be back soon enough. When you marry Jim, you can take what you want."

I looked at her and smiled. I liked the times we talked together, just her and me, even though we argued and I was set against her on the matter of Jim. "You've always got children around you, and Wood." I said.

"He's your father."

"But he likes you best," I said and Bethanna laughed. "I don't want children for awhile. I just want Jim."

"Yes, take pleasure in yourselves and know you carry the light with you, Rachel. Share it with others. Stand in the breeches of the wall wherever you find them. And there seems to be more all the time. Sometimes I think there's more breeches than wall."

Jim came up the road to have supper with us. Bethanna met and hugged him on the steps. "There's my Christian," she said.

They talked a moment.

"Yes, there was a soldier on base," Jim said. "I knew he was different from the others. He always had money. The rest of us only had it a few days after pay, then we'd be broke until we got paid again. He wasn't ever in trouble. He talked to me several times about the Lord. Then I met Rachel and I saw the same in her."

"I want to stay in Madill, Mamma," I said as we ate supper. "Pruddy said that she would stay with me."

"You are coming to Pole Cat Creek with me, Rachel," Bethanna said. "You don't take responsibility well. I've done too much for you. That's my sin, I guess. I'm going to have to be harder on you."

I had another day with Jim while Bethanna was with the lawyer, then he took Bethanna, Kemp, Cumby, and me to the train station.

"I'll see you in a year," he told me.

I rode to Pole Cat Creek with Bethanna and the others on the train. I leaned against Bethanna and sobbed when we left Jim at the station in Madill.

Even Jim had cried.

"I don't think he has known much of a family," I said, "and family is all there is in the world for me. I wonder if he would come and live with us someday—."

"No, Rachel," Mamma said. "You will go with him." She brought Grandma's old garden hat, still held it on her lap.

"It hurts to leave him behind. Now he's going to Germany for a year. He'll be alone there also."

Bethanna took my hand and looked from the window of the train with Kemp. Soon Cumby was asleep on the seat across from us. Her mouth was open and once in awhile, she twitched.

"It's the churches that make America," Bethanna

said. "Look at them everywhere we pass. We may not be as many as the unbelievers in the land, but it's us that God hears." Bethanna hummed to herself and the angels as the country passed the window, and the flat, Texas plains passed into Louisiana pines.

"Er dun't like him," Cumby said as we got off the train in Pole Cat Creek.

"Who?"

"Jim."

"Why?" Bethanna asked.

"He told me 'e would terk me fo' a ride in his jeep and 'e nuver did."

The summer months that followed were difficult. The angels throbbed with heat. We traveled to Kansas and Oklahoma with Wood. He grew despondent over his job.

"The trains are closing down," he said. "One day, even the freights will be gone."

Pole Cat Creek

In October, we returned to Louisiana. I went to school and waited for Jim's letters, which were slow in coming when he first left. I imagined myself sometimes in Germany with him. The moon over me had been over him. I wrote to him often. With so many of us in the family, there was always something to say.

When we went to church in Pole Cat Creek, Mamma cried for Mark and I cried for Jim. After Reverend Houillerie's sermon, we went to the altar and prayed for them.

On Sunday nights, we'd testify and sing.

"I just want to say that the Lord's been good to me he gave me a mamma and daddy that cared for me and I thought who knows the mind of the Lord what He'll do for us what He's working in us until He's done and then we see what He has done and I just want to praise the Lord—."

My testimonies were always short and spoken quickly because it scared me to get up in church and talk with everyone quiet and listening to what I said. And who was I with anything to say?

"Where did you get that idea, Rachel?" Mamma always said to encourage me. "You got as much to say as anyone."

And by then, Kemp and Cumby, and sometimes Andrew, were asleep on the pew in front of us with other children. Mamma always brought a neighbor with her or a railroad wife.

"My grandson," Bethanna would raise her hand when Reverend Houillerie asked who needed prayer. "The Lord knows where he is and I trust him to bring Mark back."

"The seed of the righteous shall be delivered— Proverbs eleven and twenty-one," Reverend Houillerie said. And I knew that the righteous were those covered by the blood of Jesus.

"Hedge him about, Lord," Bethanna prayed louder than anyone in church when the prayers were for Mark.

"Bless her, Lord, bless the Humes." The congregation prayed for us and for another family whose child had gone, and for men who were out of work.

"The Lord knows."

"Wooh!" voices wailed.

"The Lord be praised," Bethanna cried and afterwards we went back to our rent-house.

Les ecrevisses, the mud bugs, were once lobsters that traveled to Louisiana from Nova Scotia with the

French, and they shrank to crayfish because of the hardships of their journey.

I wrote to Jim about the Cajun tales I heard in Louisiana as I sat in the kitchen and listened to Bethanna hum and talk. The winter afternoons were damp and cold in the bayou, but Bethanna had a fire in her kitchen and neighbors and railroad wives with their children came by to talk when Wood was gone. There were always people with Bethanna. When one meal was finished, she began another. Bethanna kept children again in the afternoons. Faith and Pruddy and Cumby and I took care of them. Merrydean and Kileen were always at someone else's house or down the road in the pine woods. Sometimes my friends, Laurel and Nada, studied French with me at the kitchen table. When Wood boarded the back porch for the winter so we could have a place of our own, Laurel and Nada brought their sleeping bags and we stayed together on the back porch.

We had gone to sleep one night when I heard the loud groan of the hinge. A man came in the back door. I saw him in the cold moonlight.

He tripped over Nada and she screamed, and Laurel screamed and I was able then to scream, being at first too petrified to make a noise. I had never been so afraid. When he yelled at us to be quiet, I knew it was Mark come back after traveling on his own. It took

Bethanna the rest of the night to get the house settled again. Mark was still angry at my screaming friends and angry that he hadn't known where we were. He couldn't find us in Madill and Maclyn Howry had told him we were in Louisiana, but it must have been while we were in Kansas with Wood, because he couldn't find us and had gone on east for awhile in the fall, he told us.

I heard Bethanna humming to herself in the kitchen when the morning sun came across my face. It was because Mark was back, I remembered. Now if only Jim could come back too.

"You should go on with your studies, Rachel," Wilma, my teacher, said when she walked with me to Guibard's in Pole Cat Creek after school.

"I'm going to marry Jim Satterethwait when he comes back from Germany."

"You could do both."

"I won't be able to go to college. Wood doesn't have the money."

"There are scholarships, Rachel; you could work. I would recommend you. There's always a way to do what you want to do."

"I'm waiting for Jim," I said. I worked for Haders Guibard after school. I shelled crayfish and listened to Burdine sing. Mother made me leave at five—before the men came.

"You could go to college," Wilma said even after school was out. I sat in her house on summer mornings before I worked at Guibard's.

I thought of asking Wood one afternoon while he fished on the river if I could go to college. I looked at him in the flatboat that the Cajuns called a *pirogue*. Arthur and Wallace were between us. I never felt with Wood the way I did with Bethanna, but I couldn't ask her about college either.

It sounded reasonable when Wilma talked to me, but it was unspeakable when I looked at Wood in the flatboat as we passed under the heavy trees along the river.

Madill, Texas

Jim would be a corporal when he returned from Germany, he wrote, and we would be stationed at Fort Cobb in Muleshoe, Louisiana. I went to Madill a week before he came back. Mamma Bethanna wrote Maclyn Howry to stay with me in Grandma's house. Everyone was in school in Pole Cat Creek. It was the first year I could remember that I didn't start back to school.

Before I left, Mamma finished my wedding dress with the thin lace from the collar and sleeves of Grandma's other good dress, the one she wasn't buried in. Jim would bring my veil from Germany.

A neighbor took me to the base the afternoon Jim was to get in. The plane was delayed and I waited until late at night. I thought it must be the turbulent weather in the Gulf. I slept awhile on a bench and when I woke, I heard the roar of a plane. Confused a moment, I sat up and knew that Jim was coming.

Bethanna and Wood and the children rode the train through the night for the wedding. It was the last ride from Louisiana back to the far plains of Texas. The passenger car was going to be taken from the train.

After Bethanna got the children settled, we sat for awhile on the porch. Then I went to the plum bushes for my last time as a girl.

The next morning, the sky was dark. The angels were arguing in the corner of the room.

When we drove to the Madill Grace Church, the clouds had reached from the storm in the Gulf far inland to our wedding. Thunder roared and lightning ripped the sky. A gust of wind sent the rain smell into the church. It made goosebumps on my arms.

It was a late summer storm kicking at the church, chugging like the last of the passenger cars. I saw Wood look toward the south too. Lightning scorched the air.

Jim came into the church with the veil he brought from Germany and put it on my head. The wedding ceremony began quickly at the Madill Grace Church with my family standing around us and the guests sitting behind us in the pews. Jim's parents had come from Riler, Texas.

I carried a twig of the plum bush.

Arthur, Mark, Wallace, and soldiers from Fort Jether ushered with my brothers. They closed the windows of the church as the rain stampeded. I held Jim's hand as though we would be run over in the church on the wide prairie.

"Sometimes we just hold on to our saddle and go where the horse goes," Reverend Danner said in the middle of the ceremony. I heard nervous laughter between the thunder claps and looked around at the men with their arms around their wives. Faith and Pruddy held on to one another and Cumby ran to Bethanna. I thought any moment Reverend Danner would tell us to crawl under the pews.

I couldn't hear what Reverend Danner said in the loud claps of thunder. Suddenly a child screamed. I covered my face and ran to Bethanna.

She held me a moment, then nudged me away. "Rachel. Rachel. Go back to Jim."

Reverend Danner and the others waited for me to come back to the altar under the small hand of the church over us in the storm.

When I stood beside Jim again, he didn't take my hand. Revenend Danner continued the vows. Jim said them quietly and my repeating of them was quiet too.

Jim lifted the veil and kissed me when the ceremony was over. We had cake in the back room of the church and Reverend Danner's wife played hymns on the piano. We sang until the hard, steady rain let up enough that we could leave the church.

I hugged Bethanna and the others and gave the twig of plum blossom to Faith.

The highway was as dark as the storm clouds.

"I thought you wanted to marry me," Jim said when we were alone on the road.

"I did. I do," I said.

"You ran to your mother."

"I was afraid. I'm sorry, Jim."

He didn't say anything but after awhile he took my hand as I watched the road signs that passed into dark.

Cayuga.

Rye.

Port Arthur.

We drove to Fort Cobb in Muleshoe, Louisiana, where Jim was stationed, the angels waving before us the windshield wipers of their hands.

Fort Cobb, Louisiana

I could drive the jeep to Bethanna's house in Pole Cat Creek in two hours. I stayed with her during the day and visited with the children.

In the evening, I was back at Fort Cobb making supper for Jim, telling about my day with Bethanna.

Then after the summer, I was sick and Bethanna said I was going to have a baby.

"I just know the Lord will be with me, being good to me and all." Wallace and Cumby turned from their pew in Reverend Houillerie's church in Pole Cat Creek and stared at me as though I were someone other than their sister. Bethanna, Wood, and the children were going back to Madill for the winter. I could hear the angels like bees under the pews looking for a place for the winter. "I praise the Lord for my family and my husband," I said, "and the baby He is going to give me and the Lord's been good to me," but I choked on my tears as I finished talking and sat down beside Bethanna and cried as she held her arm around me.

"I can't go with you, Bethanna?"

"No," she said. "Hedge her about, Lord."

"Bless her, Lord," they prayed.

Jim's friends came to our small barracks and I sat in the smoke-filled room. I was uncomfortable carrying the baby and irritable. They talked about nothing in which I was interested. I wanted to be in the plum bushes in Madill with Bethanna and the others. I wanted to be at the river in Pole Cat Creek, Louisiana, when they returned there. We'd sing and talk, and I'd be under Bethanna's arm with the red firelight jumping in our faces—and would always jump, I had thought— and it was all there had to be.

I thought of Esmus and Wolfer, Roy and Virgil, when I heard Jim's friends in the barracks. The girls smoked and I didn't know what to talk to them about. They slept with other men, talked of it when their husbands weren't listening, and I wanted them to leave.

Then I was in the army hospital with Jim having his baby which I lived through, though later I knew I almost died and didn't remember the three months afterwards that I'd been sick. It was Madill where I was again, or the firelight in the Louisiana bayou. It felt like cotton in my hands. I touched Bethanna and the river. Wood, Arthur, Faith, Pruddy—but it was the light of Jesus coming down like campfire—or the headlights of Wood's truck on the road. And I thought that if I were dying then I would, for it was the edge of the river at Pole Cat Creek.

Call upon Jesus they said. Jesus. Jesus. I thought it must be Burdine wailing as she always did. I looked at the fire and felt His arms pulling me back from Madill, and I didn't think He knew what He was doing, and I said, Jesus. It was Him. Pole Cat Creek and summer nights with crayfish and Bethanna's arm around me. It was God that had given me and I was to give to Him the child. Had he been born? It seemed strange that I had a child. I wondered how old he was, and cold, still with Bethanna by the river. I listened to Burdine wail. Cumby asked what was all that noise she was making, and Bethanna told Cumby to go back to sleep and not to think about it.

I tried to wake because Pole Cat Creek was drowning me. I choked and said go to Madill Bethanna as if it were Texas. Jim was there, and Bethanna's arm was around me in the firelight of Pole Cat Creek. I heard Jim sobbing and looked at the bare-awful walls where I was and cried that we could be under the trees leaning to the river and fish on the end of the pole and the flicker of firelight in the distance. I saw Bess again and asked where the children were but she couldn't hear me. Mark I said and thought she was looking for him.

Bethanna's arms came for me again in the campfire. The noise of nightbugs in the swamp was like planes at the base, Jim said the planes, Rachel, can't you hear?

Then Hume moved on with the railroad and we left Pole Cat Creek, but anywhere we were there was Bethanna, and the road signs passing the truck.

Madill.

Poteau.

Nacogdoches.

We lived in Texas towns the wind carried away but for Bethanna's prayers. We lived in the Louisiana bayou where the land sank into swamps and rusted Wood's tools. And there were churches in the towns and woodfires at night. Bethanna could cook and make beds for us anywhere.

She was the only piece of furniture in the house.

People were always in her kitchen. She would talk and laugh and see my Rachel, she said when I was married and the baby first showed.

Bethanna.

She's not here. He sounded angry, and I opened my eyes and looked at him. "Rachel, do you see me?" Jim was there when I came back to the bare room from Pole Cat Creek. I wanted the river and Bethanna's arms. They said I had a boy and even Burdine said. I looked at those testifying in Madill Grace Church and we sang while the campfire jumped. Bethanna held Beth Howry's garden hat.

"Yas, Lord," they said. *"Mon Dieu."*

I felt the buttons on her coat.

Jim was on the back row of the church, Cumby said, and I turned and saw him. "Berth 'then doo," she said but I couldn't understand her. Bethanna said I could go, but I had swallowed a fishbone and she pounded me on the back I thought I would choke on the button of her coat but I kept gasping for air tearing at the water in Pole Cat Creek I was drowning again how could a person breathe with a button in their throat and the waters of Pole Cat Creek over their head and I beat for air.

What do army doctors know about women? I heard Jim's voice as clear as Bethanna's. But they didn't know that the other was there. I hid in the plum bushes when the planes went over.

Jim's voice was clear. Bethanna had been crying and Kemp frowned and I turned to see if Jim was there. "He's on the back row, Bethanna," I said. "Can I go?" She said, yes, but my feet wouldn't move. And I was stationed at the army base. She said I could go and she was there shaking her head at Jim. She'd told me I could go to him.

Bess was in the hall again. I told her we had the children but I couldn't think if Mark was back and I had to say I didn't know but she was busy then with someone else and couldn't talk. I stayed in the plum bushes in Grandma's backyard thinking if Mark had come and whirlibirds from the base flew over and Wallace and Andrew ran screaming through the backyard flying when the helicopter flew over and the column of army trucks went by. They were going to be flown to a hospital. Jim came in the plum bushes to tell me.

"Okay," I said.

He said Jim. It's Jim. He came in to tell me he was Jim. Hang on Rachel he said in the plum bushes he said it again but I could not. There was something over my face and Bethanna blowing my nose it was Faith and Cumby in bed with me against Kileen's arm and she wouldn't move over I could hardly breathe and pushed them away and they wouldn't.

"It's Jim. I'm with you. Don't fight, Rachel. She can't come. I'm here with you. We're going to the hospital in Shreveport."

Jim was there did he get back from Germany? He put the wedding veil over my face but I had to find Mark for Bess I told him. He never knew. I thought of Jim in the plum bushes down the road the noise of the helicopters I was afraid the wind blew my veil over my face in Pole Cat Creek the water over me. Jim took my hand. I choked. I knew it was him to get the button. I tried to take the veil down but he held it on coughing.

I said it clearly.

Tell him, Bethanna, I can't breathe with it.

"She doesn't give up," I heard Jim's voice and told him I could hear and knew it was him.

But the angels had wings now that flew over their heads. They were floating waves as if I were in Pole Cat Creek their faces bare white when I looked too close at the angels said back up. I can't see to fly with you the angels were talking. They said wait not yet and they wouldn't let me where I wanted they wouldn't let me around them but pushed back with their hands on my chest their rough flight I said angels should be able to get somewhere but I couldn't see around they held out their cheeks and were like clouds that wouldn't let me pass.

Jim told me later I'd hemorrhaged after the baby was born and then had pneumonia. The baby was already three months old and I wouldn't be able to have other children because I had surgery that I couldn't remember.

But I remembered the afternoon my mind came together and I saw Jim standing at the window. I called to him and he turned to me.

"Did you call Jim?" he asked. He stood looking at me. "Do you see me, Rachel?"

"Yes. I have before now, and when we came on the plane yesterday I knew it was you."

"It was a helicopter four weeks ago."

I had to remember Jim, and I loved him and had begged Bethanna to let me be with him. He was the one I had wanted to be with. I had to keep that in my mind. I looked at him several times trying to remember and he asked me what was the matter. I felt like I didn't know him sometimes and I was with a stranger. He was the soldier at Fort Jether I met long ago and it had turned out badly.

Now I was talking to him again, and I didn't know why we were together for some reason and Bethanna was not here.

"Where is she?" I asked.

"She's been sick," he answered. A pain of dread went through me. "Is she dead?"

"No. She just is not able to travel. I've taken the baby to Madill. Faith and Kileen and Cumby and Pruddy take care of him. I left him with a couple on the base for awhile but they were getting tired of him and I couldn't afford to pay them anyway. My mother came for awhile too but it was hard for her and she left."

"The baby?"

"Jeremy." Jim buried his head on my chest and sobbed. "Rachel, I didn't think you'd live." He called for the nurses, and I cried that Bethanna had been sick and I wasn't with her and now she had my child like she had Bess's.

I was ready to get up but I couldn't move. I trembled with weakness. It was because I had been in bed so long, the doctor said. It would take awhile to get my strength back. He asked my name. He had me count. I slept awhile and woke up with the doctor and nurses and Jim still over me.

He was laughing as I said my name again and where I was and who he was though I didn't know what day it was. Time was something that had disappeared for awhile.

"You didn't know me, Rachel. You were still with Bethanna before we were married." Jim went to call Reverend Danner in Madill. He would go to Bethanna's house and tell them that I was going to be all right.

I wondered again what had happened as I went back to sleep in a red light that came in the room. I was going to have a baby and it was gone. I couldn't feel its hump in my stomach anymore and its name was Jeremy. A friend of Jim's had kept it for awhile and now it was in Madill.

Jim had to go back to the base in the morning.

When Jim returned to the hospital in Shreveport from the army base, he told me about Bethanna's illness. Then she called me in the hospital from the Madill Grace Church. When I heard her voice, it was like the first light when I peeped out of a cave. "Bethanna. Bethanna," I quivered at the sound of her voice. I felt life again as we talked, sometimes not speaking for moments because of the sob in my throat that we were both alive.

"I cried your name a hundred times, Jim told me." Then Bethanna cried because she hadn't been able to be with me. "It was the Lord that kept me from you, Rachel," she said, "so that you would lean on Jim and not me."

But I didn't think it could be true.

"I hated her for awhile," Jim said after Bethanna and I talked, "because she was the one you called for."

Cumby had been sick too and Bethanna said that she had trouble with Mark. He had gone off again, but Wood had gone after him and brought him back to Madill. Now that her mamma was dead, she didn't have anyone to help her with the kids. Maclyn Howry was too old. Faith was going to be married and she didn't have her mind on helping Mamma.

Kileen and Pruddy would bring Jeremy back to the base in Louisiana when I was able to return to Fort Cobb, but I only wanted to be with Bethanna in Madill again.

In two weeks I went back to the army base. I slept most of the time and was hardly aware of Kileen and Pruddy when they came with Jeremy. I could hear their voices in the barracks but was often not concerned with them. I would look at Jeremy during the meals and have to remind myself he was mine. When Kileen and Pruddy left, I still didn't have any strength. I slept several times a day. Usually, I slept as much as Jeremy.

Sometimes I sat in the chair to feed him and cried.

Jim hit the table with his fist when he came in the barracks one afternoon. "What am I supposed to do?" he asked. He pounded the table, pounded it and pounded it until Jeremy screamed with fright and I cried at Jim to stop.

"What am I supposed to do with a wife who cries all day?" Jim turned from the table and stomped out the door. Afterwards, Jim got a woman to stay with us. He paid her what he could. She was a Christian woman, and she said the Lord would pay her what we couldn't.

I wanted to be a pillar like Bethanna but I couldn't get through the morning without napping. Then a neighbor took Jeremy for a day or two while I sat in the chair with the shawl over me and held my head in my hands. Jim cleaned when he came back at night. I didn't have the strength to get up. I couldn't remember one day from another. I couldn't cook anything for Jim to eat without having to go back to bed.

When he couldn't see me, I cried over the plainness of the army barracks, and I cried at not having anyone to talk to. Bethanna left the room empty. Nothing could fill it. It took all my energy one night to bake Jim an apple pie. I went to bed shortly afterwards, too tired to eat or clean up the table. I didn't know what was wrong and I couldn't tell Jim. Leaves piled up outside the barracks' window. The sun was red, always red and it snapped like a beetle against the glass at night. SSSShhhhh! I said to it. I didn't want Jim to know. I would rake the leaves in my dreams and hit the sun when it darted into the barracks.

The army nursery took Jeremy when he was six months old. Even that cost money and I knew we didn't have it. I didn't ask Jim about the doctor bills. He was pale and hardly smiled, even when Jeremy cooed to him.

"It will take seven years to get even, then another seven," he said.

Jim took me to the chaplain when I didn't get better. I talked to the man about what I could remember of the months I was in the hospital. I told him about Bethanna. I read him a letter Cumby wrote in her large print. Even Arthur had sent a note. But I didn't tell him sometimes the walls of the barracks and the yard were red. I didn't tell him sometimes the angels hissed.

"Are you unhappy because you can't have more children?" Chaplain Gustafson asked.

I had always had children around me. The house was empty without them. I thought about that a moment and felt homesick again. "No. I can always have children. My mother took them in, still does when she's not sick, and I thought of doing that too. I've seen children around the barracks that need care, but I don't feel like it now. I can always find children—but it's having the responsibility of them without Bethanna who made everything fun. It's having to originate everything I do by myself," I began crying, "and finding it all so empty—."

The chaplain didn't say anthing.

"I want to retreat into Bethanna and never come out. Nothing else makes any difference. I want the campfire burning before my eyes. I want forever to be at Bethanna's side. That's the only place anything happens. Not out here by myself in this cave that's so hollow I can't find walls to touch when I hold out my arms. And if anyone comes to visit, which I don't want them to, they ask what is the matter and I say I would like to visit my mother and they say that that's what they came to get away from. They think I'm crazy. I don't have any of them for friends. I don't want any of them. I'm tired when I wake up. I have to fix Jim's breakfast and he just looks at his plate and eats. I get dizzy and the baby is there crying unless Jim takes him to the nursery. He says he does enough and when can I start taking care of my own child when he's had the reponsibility of him since he was born. I have to go back to bed when Jim is gone, crying and wondering who this baby is that is always with me and why I can't be with Bethanna."

"What do you do when you go back to bed?"

"I sleep and forget what I feel like. I forget that I shrank from the hardship of the journey and remember what it was like when I was still with Bethanna." I told Chaplain Gustafson about Nada and Laurel, my friends in Pole Cat Creek, and Wilma, my teacher, and the Cajun tales they told.

"You and Jim have had a hard time. You have to expect it to show up in your marriage. But many people I talk to have a hard time. Many of them, Rachel, have a harder time than you. Living in the army barracks is grim. There are medical bills from when you were taken to Shreveport and no longer in the army infirmary. Jim has the feeling he'll never be able to pay them. I know your lives seem frustrating at the moment. But you have a stable background to draw on. You should be able to get through—."

"But I can't," I interrupted him. "Instead it draws me until I can't go on without it. Sometimes I look at the plates and pots I brought from Grandma's house and I cry."

"Do you want to go back to Pole Cat Creek and visit your teacher and friends?"

I paused a moment. "No. Laurel and Nada have gone to school and I don't want Wilma to see me either, pale and thin like I am now. I don't like to see myself in the mirror."

"Would you like to go to Madill and visit your mother?"

I jumped from the chair. "Yes!" I screamed. "Yes!"

"Jim and I have talked about it and he's agreed," Chaplain Gustafson said. "I've written your mother. Maybe a visit will put some life into you. I can see, Rachel, why it draws you—."

I went back to the barracks and got my suitcase and put my two dresses into it, which didn't fit anyway because I was too thin. I would work at The Old Dime Box and buy some clothes. I would talk to Bethanna late into the night and spend Saturdays with Faith and

Pruddy. I clapped my hands together as I felt my strength come back to me. I felt like I had long, long ago. I straightened the barracks and packed Jeremy's belongings in an army duffle bag. When Jim came in I told him we were going to Madill!

He knew it also and looked tired. I couldn't understand why he wasn't happy. He'd been given a short furlough and we were leaving Fort Cobb. A hissing angel came in the window and I swatted it away with my arm.

The bus came into the station in Muleshoe, Louisiana, near Fort Cobb. I wanted to take the train and feel the ground rumble under me when it came into the station and smell the train-smell I had always known. But the passenger cars had been taken off. I thought I would burst when I got on the bus. Everything else, I knew, would be the same. The highway would connect with Bethanna, just as the train tracks did. I was going to MADILL. Everyone had to be from somewhere. And I was from Madill, Texas.

I cried most of the way—I asked if we were across the Red River before we left Louisiana. I wanted my head on Bethanna's bosom and her arms around me. I had never been away from her so long and never wanted to be again. I had gone to Fort Cobb and nearly died. Now I was going to Madill.

MADILL! I felt like I had when we'd been away and Wood came in and said we were going to Madill, and we were all together in Wood's truck, laughing.

Jim handed me the baby.

"Are we in Texas yet?"

"We're almost to the Red River," he said.

Bethanna was surrounded by Wood and the children and neighbors when we came into the bus station. I didn't see her at first and panicked.

"She's there, Rachel," Jim said. "She's all right."

"BETHANNA!" I screamed climbing down the stairs of the bus, shoving past the people in front of me, making them angry, but I wanted to reach Bethanna. I screamed again when I reached her. We wailed and cried and all the neighbors and children carried on something terrible.

"Good God, Rachel." Jim said. But I thought I would burst when I hugged Bethanna.

Faith and Cumby rushed to the baby and took him from me. He was screaming in terror anyway, not understanding what was happening.

"Er think yeud gone enver cum back—the nartacks gert yeu," Cumby yelled at me.

"Yes —," I smoothed her head and saw that Beth-anna had been sick when I looked at her.

She was pale and I saw how plain she looked. She must have thought the same of me because we cried and hugged again.

"We've been through a lot," she said and took Jim in her arms too. "This one has been our strength," she said.

Wood made several trips to take us from the bus station to Grandma's house. I waved to the neighbors as we left, then finally, FINALLY, we were in Grandma's house shut away from Fort Cobb and everything terrible that had happened. We changed Jeremy and fed him and rocked him to sleep.

Bethanna showed me the christening dress she was making for him.

I didn't feel like going to the church at the base. We would have Jeremy baptized at the Madill Grace Church.

Bethanna told me Mark was gone again. Maclyn Howry had grown tired of the noise in Grandma's house and went back to her own place. Wallace's father had come back for him after all these years and wanted him. Bethanna was afraid she was going to lose him too. Then Faith would be getting married.

"Where's Jim?" Merrydean asked as Bethanna and I talked on the back porch.

"I don't know," I said. "I haven't seen him."

In the days that followed, I was drunk with Madill. I walked into town. Cumby pushed the baby. I went to The Old Dime Box, and they looked at Jeremy and said I could come back to work if I wanted. I laughed with Bethanna into the night at the long table in the kitchen. Her mamma's garden hat was on the peg of the wall. We almost looked like ourselves again, Wood told us smiling.

"Go out with me," Jim said. "Let's go to town."

"I want to stay with Mamma."

"Damn it, Rachel," he yelled. "You aren't your mamma's anymore. You're my wife. It's been a long time without you."

I smelled beer on his breath.

"It isn't the first time," Faith said after Jim left.

"What is it?" I asked.

Wood was looking at me.

"Jim needs you."

"He's all right."

"No, he isn't, Rachel. I've seen him at Stojo's. He needs you."

For a moment the thought of Jerusha Harwood crossed my mind, but I was soon talking to Bethanna again.

Jim went back to Fort Cobb when his furlough was up.

Madill, Texas

Reverend Danner came to the house one afternoon. I knew he came to talk to me.

"I want to have Jeremy baptized on Sunday," I told him.

"We'll wait until Jeremy's father can be with us," he stated. "You're withdrawn, Rachel," he started on what I knew he'd come to talk about. "I can see it in your face."

I laughed. "I've already talked to Chaplain Gustafson about that. I shrank with the hardships of the journey," I said, "like the crayfish."

He went on. "If you hold back, you'll ruin your marriage and your child's chance of life with both his parents."

Cumby sat by me and looked at us as we talked. The doctor had told Bethanna that she was retarded and I stroked her head.

"I remember you in love with Jim," Reverend Danner said.

I reddened and looked at my fingers in my lap.

"I remember several prayer meetings at church

when Bethanna prayed for you and Jim. Now you're back with Bethanna not two years later?"

"I nearly died."

"I know, Rachel. I think it was Bethanna's faith that held you here. I gave up several times when I talked to Jim and the doctor. But you lived."

"I don't like the army base," I told Reverend Danner. "I'm tired all the time. I don't like the barracks, and I don't like the responsibility of being by myself with Jeremy. I've never been alone. I miss Bethanna desperately. I forgave her for not coming to me only when I got back and saw she'd been sick too."

"She couldn't afford to come to you either. She's still paying for phone bills from the church while you were sick." Reverend Danner paused. "You clung to Bethanna instead of Jim. He's your husband. You have work to do, Rachel, on the army base where you're stationed now—and wherever you'll be stationed."

Jeremy cried from the other room and Cumby got up from the couch beside me.

"I always thought Bethanna was the perfect mother, but I saw Bess, and now you, and probably Faith unable to adjust to marriage, to adjust to any life away from Bethanna and the family."

"I nearly died with Jeremy," I explained to Reverend Danner again. "It takes a while to get over that."

"Isn't Jeremy nearly a year old now?"

"Yes."

"And you're still dying, Rachel. You ought to be at Fort Cobb with Jim."

I looked impatiently out the window. "I don't like it there. It's empty and I'm alone. It is hard to be without Bethanna."

I knew Bethanna stayed in the garden because she wanted me to listen to Reverend Danner.

"You had a good upbringing, Rachel. Maybe too good. Maybe so good you can't grow up because you'd have to leave it," he said. "But God will be what Bethanna has been to you."

I struggled to listen to Reverend Danner but I didn't want to hear him.

"I hope all the time that Wood will come back to Pole Cat Creek and I'll be able to be with Bethanna most of the day."

"Do you think she's had better places to live than the barracks? Let the love you've known show in the army camp. Bethanna has done everything for you. You were nothing on your own without her. That's the terrible discovery you've made. She was your reason for living. You could attach yourself to her side and ride through life. You never had to look within yourself for anything. Now you have to find the strength to live. That's your terrible crisis, Rachel. The reason you're tired."

"I am not so tired here."

"Yes, because you're back with Bethanna. You're still a girl here and Jeremy is more like your brother. Others are caring for him. And Jim, whom you loved and married and should be living with and giving to him and Jeremy the love that Bethanna gave you, is back at Fort Cobb."

Cumby came back to the couch and sat with me again.

"Whenever I closed my eyes, I saw Bethanna and Pole Cat Creek and Madill and Bethanna again with the children around her," I said. "The army base is nothing like that. You wouldn't like the people there," I told Reverend Danner. "They drink and smoke pot and sleep with other people."

"What kind of people do you think Jesus was around?" he asked me. "Or is it that you can't fit in anywhere outside of Bethanna? That was Bess also. She lived protected by Bethanna. When Bethanna was gone, and she was by herself, she had nothing. Tragedy followed her like it does Mark, like it will you if you don't find your own light from within, Rachel, and that light comes from our Lord Jesus Christ."

"Just what I expected a minister to say," I said.

"Give your light to Jim and Jeremy and the others—neighbors and all those people sleeping with other people. That light in you was what attracted Jim

in the first place. But you were only reflecting Bethanna," Reverend Danner was listening to himself talk. I
thought for a moment he was in his pulpit. "Do you go
to church in Louisiana?"

"Sometimes. When I feel like it. Not often," I
said. "There's a chapel on base."

"Is Gustafson the minister, the one I talked to?"

"Yes."

"Is there a church in Muleshoe you'd like?"

"I don't know."

"Why don't you look there for a church?" he said.
"Do you have a Bible study in your barracks?"

I laughed. "Do you know what they'd say if I
suggested that?"

"Have you ever?"

"No."

"Has anyone?"

"Not that I know of."

"Why don't you begin one on Friday nights?"

"They do other things on Friday nights. I don't
think it would appeal to them. Even Jim."

"Rachel, whether you know it or not, it was Jim
who held onto you as much as Bethanna when you were
sick. I saw his faith grow as I talked to him on the phone
those months," Reverend Danner explained. "If he
doesn't want a Bible study, have one with the women.

You'll find other Christian women there if you just look."

"I don't want to," I said, and Cumby looked at me.

"You would rather stay with Bethanna?"

"Yes. I don't like being in four closet-rooms with a small child. I never knew we didn't have money when I was with Bethanna and Wood. Now I know I don't have money, and I don't like it. I want to be in Madill with the Humes."

"Yes, Rachel," Reverend Danner said. "When you want to grow up I'll talk to you again."

"I don't like Reverend Danner," I said when Bethanna came in the house from the garden and he was gone. "He's old."

"I know," Bethanna said. "He has talked to me also, Rachel. Faith is getting married and he said I was to have my third daughter fail at trying to make a marriage."

"Don't let him in the house. Why do you go to his church?"

"Because he's right. I was angry with him too. I said words to him that I wish I hadn't, but I did. But I've kept in mind what he said. You aren't my child any longer, Rachel. I need all of you around me too. But I can't have you to myself. You belong to Jim now.

Without knowing it, I crippled you as I raised you."
Bethanna broke into a sob at the table.

"That's not true," I said.

Cumby cried too and I felt my anger against
Reverend Danner again.

"The family has to be a fortress against the world.
But I cut off every way out. My place was not to keep
you safe but to provide you with the strength to build
your own fort. I've gone to Reverend Danner a long
time, Rachel, to talk to him. I've been going since you
had Jeremy and I was sick and couldn't go to you. Wood
agrees—."

"I don't."

"And Cumby, precious little thing, has always seen
too much and doesn't understand what she sees." Bethanna held her. "I cried when I saw what I'd done to you."

"You didn't do anything to me, Mamma, but give
me love. Don't listen to them."

Bethanna sighed and wiped her eyes.

I walked out of the house and went to the plum
bushes. Jeremy saw me and cried to come, but I told
Kileen to hold him. I sat in the plum bushes awhile and
cried. I had to make my own place; I remembered
Bethanna's words. I had gone to Fort Cobb in love with
Jim Satterethwait. He was all I had wanted. But after
Bethanna moved from Pole Cat Creek and Jim was all I
had, there wasn't much to hold us together.

"It would have been better if I died, Mamma," I said when I came back into the house.

"Don't talk that way."

"I'm bored at Fort Cobb. When I drove past the road that went to the highway where I could start toward Madill or Pole Cat Creek, I would cry. I want to be with you, Bethanna. When I cook meals with you, I don't realize I'm cooking. Your kitchen has children laughing and neighbors talking and the taste and smell of your eggplant and tomatoes and squash. But when I'm on my own, the barracks are ugly. I hear neighbors yelling and cursing. It's a chore to get a meal on the table and I'm tired afterwards." I wiped my eyes on the hem of my dress. "Why is it that way?" I asked but she didn't say anything. "I want to fish in Pole Cat Creek and smell your Cajun bread. I want to be at the table laughing with you all. I want to see Kemp's frown, and I want to be with you when Wallace's father comes to him. Jim is different than us, Bethanna," I said. "He doesn't talk when he eats. He just eats. When I want Jim, I want him here with us."

Bethanna smiled. "I understand what you say, Rachel. I even understand Bess more than I did, and I'm already talking to Faith about what she is going to face. But you can't stay here, Rachel, even with Jim. The time has come for you to leave and you will be able to."

"I can't be like you, Bethanna, giving yourself to everyone."

"You have Jesus, Rachel, and you're not alone."

"I won't go," I insisted. "Even the sun there is glaring and hard and always red—."

"You will, Rachel," Bethanna interrupted. "You can't stay here. Wood has already decided that."

"My own father?"

"Yes."

"But I can work at The Old Dime Box and pay him for my keep. I could even rent the room above the store."

"You couldn't earn enough to pay rent and buy groceries and pay babysitting," Bethanna said. "I wanted you to have something you could do, Rachel, but that's not for you. You've got too much feeling. You need Jim and Jeremy—you seem to be happy in the mess of house and children. How could you expect Jim to be like us? He wasn't raised like you, Rachel. Be patient with him."

Wood came into the kitchen. He must have been listening from the other room like Grandma used to do.

"Madill isn't anywhere but in you, Rachel. And Pole Cat Creek is just a muddy river."

"Maybe to you," I said. "But it's got the biggest crayfish in Louisiana."

He laughed. "We've had it good."

"So good I can't leave."

"Arthur will take you back to Fort Cobb when you're ready."

"I'm not ready."

"Maybe Cumby could come with you for awhile to help you with Jeremy."

I drove to the edge of Madill, past the gate to the cow pasture where I'd been with Jim. I felt a stirring of the passion I had with him. Not the way it was at first but after I got used to him. It was gone when I got back to Bethanna's house, but passing the place again one day with Jeremy and Cumby in Wood's truck, I felt it again. I wanted to be with Jim. It was time I left Bethanna but I couldn't yet. I hadn't felt good since I had been pregnant with Jeremy. It had been almost two years ago. But now I was healed. I couldn't have any more children. It wouldn't happen again. If I had gone to the doctor before I got married, or when I was first pregnant, maybe he would have seen the problem and it could have been prevented or lessened.

"What if he could get a transfer back to Fort Jether," I said.

"No," Wood answered. I was Jim's wife and would go where he was.

"It will be all right," Bethanna said. "You make his meals and clean the house. That's what's in you. Love and care for your family."

I slammed the door and went to the plum bushes again.

"It's not fair," I said to Bethanna later.

"Our work is returned, Rachel. They aren't complete without us either. We have what they lack. It brings them back from Stojo's again and again."

"It makes me mad, though, Mamma, that things are that way. I think sometimes I'd like to be like Jerusha Harwood."

"But you've got what she wants, Rachel."

"Yes, but she won't pay the price."

"Do you love Jim, Rachel?" Reverend Danner asked when I went to see him before I went back to Fort Cobb.

"Yes. I know love changes. And I almost lost it. But I think it is still there, if I dig down through all that has happened."

Reverend Danner was quiet as he listened to me and I knew he was thinking about something. "I want to talk to you, Rachel," he said. "I thought at first I wouldn't, but that would be protecting you just like Bethanna has always done. I've got something to tell you and you won't like it." He paused again. "It will be another turning point in the crisis you've been through."

"What is it, then?" I asked impatiently.

"Jim has been living with another woman at Fort Cobb while you've been in Madill. You can't have Arthur drive you back without telling Jim you're coming."

My mouth hung open. "How do you know?"

"I've talked with him several times. Jim loves you, Rachel, but you left him and there is always someone to fill the place you vacate. You left Jim for your mother. He didn't leave you. I can't blame him. I can't condone adultery, but I can understand Jim. I love him also. He was saved in my church. I've talked to him through the months you were critical. You called for Bethanna and not him. That was hard for him. You haven't realized what you've done to him. You rejected his love. He is in debt because of your medical bills. Maybe he's been through more than you have. He didn't have you—and another woman offered him her love. He needed it."

"Who is it?" I asked angrily.

"That's not the point. You didn't want him, Rachel. Did you think he could endure Fort Cobb without you? He's known your love just as you've known Bethanna's. How do you think he felt—."

"It's Jerusha Harwood with her crimped hair," I said.

"Rachel—."

"They were together before I knew him. And

when he didn't come to Bethanna's mamma's house, I always knew he was with her." I hit my hand on his desk, enraged that he'd been having her all these weeks I'd been in Madill. How dare them! In the same barracks where I had lived with him! With Grandma's belongings in there with them! I raged and got up to rush from his office, but he held my arm. I looked at him surprised but he wouldn't let go of my arm. He was an old minister, and for one minute, I wanted to push him aside. I hit the desk again with my hand when he let go of my arm.

"You do love him, Rachel."

"He's my husband," I cried. "I don't like her. Especially her."

"Write Jim a letter. You can't go unannounced."

"Why not?"

"You left of your own accord."

"I can go back of my own accord. She can get out."

"Jim asked her to come with him. He will have to ask her to leave. He doesn't know you want to come back. You've shown him you don't want him," Reverend Danner said. "You write to him, Rachel, if you want to go back."

Jim. I was wrong and would like another chance to be your wife. Rachel Hume Satterethwait.

"That's quite a letter," Reverend Danner said.

"It's all I can do at the moment."

"Do you want to wait and write later?"

"And give her longer to be with him?" I nearly shouted at Reverend Danner.

"The letter will do," he said.

I didn't hear anything from Jim for two weeks. I wanted to go back to Fort Cobb and throw Jerusha Harwood out of my barracks. But I had gone long periods of time without thinking about Jim, Reverend Danner reminded me. I could wait for him.

"Shucks." I had washed Arthur's windbreaker with his leather pilot's gloves still in the pockets. "They're probably ruined, Arthur. I'm sorry. I forgot about looking in the pockets."

"Jim called while you were at the laundry."

"What did he say, Arthur?" I asked him quickly.

"It wasn't me he wanted to talk to. He asked for you. I told him you'd be back in an hour."

"Why didn't you come to the laundry to get me?" I went to the door to go to the phone at the church.

"Wait for him to call you, Rachel," Bethanna said.

"How long has it been?"

"Maybe an hour," Arthur said.

"He should be calling," I sorted nervously through the clothes. "It's too hard, Bethanna," I said impatiently. "I can't tell anymore what belongs to who. I'll take Jeremy's clothes and you sort the rest."

Jim didn't call until the next day and I was beside myself. I wanted to call but Bethanna wouldn't let me. "He'll come to you," she said.

"While Jerusha gets him again tonight?"

"Rachel. He waited for you a long time and you never came around."

"I have now and I want him."

"Shame, Rachel. There's children here. Watch what you say."

"I'm angry."

"Jim's here," Pruddy said rushing in from the porch.

I ran to the door. He stood on the porch with his hands to his side. Cumby stood staring at him.

I opened the door and kissed him. He still stood with his hands to his sides.

"Jim," I said.

The kids gathered around us. One of the boys carried Jeremy. Jim took him and tossed him in the air. Jeremy screamed with delight. It was the first time Jim smiled since he came on the porch. Jeremy laughed and Cumby did then also.

Jim looked at me not knowing what to say because there was so much to say.

"Come out on the back porch. Maybe there won't be anyone there," I said.

Jim shook hands with Wood. Bethanna hugged Jim and took Jeremy. She called Cumby when she started to follow us. I turned to Jim on the porch and waited for him to kiss me.

"Rachel, I've come to talk to you."

"I know about Jerusha," I said.

He held me back from holding him. "I've been happy with her," he said.

"Why did you come then?" I wasn't ready for his words.

"To see you, Rachel, and Jeremy. You're my wife. I loved you but it all went wrong. I couldn't compete with Madill and your mother. I won't ever be able to."

"But I've come to myself, Jim," I said. "It took a long time." I put my hand to his cheek. He didn't resist and I kissed him.

"Don't, Rachel," he said. "I need time to decide other than this way. I came to ask for a divorce, but I still care for you." He held me in his arms. "Jerusha stayed with me, Rachel. We had a good time."

"You've already said that. I heard you the first time. I am your wife and Jeremy is your child."

"It's taken you a while to realize that."

"Give me another chance."

"I'll be in town," he turned to leave.

"No. That's giving her another chance."

"Rachel. I've lived with her."

"You've lived with me longer."

"I have to explain to her."

"No you don't. She's had other soldiers—."

"Shut up, Rachel," he said and left the porch. I ran after him through the kitchen. He hugged Jeremy and left. There was nothing I could do to stop him.

I thought he'd be back for dinner. I had a place set for him beside me at the long table.

But he didn't come. I wanted several times to go to town but Bethanna stood in my way.

"She's talking him into staying with her," I cried.

"I don't think you should run after him, Rachel. You can only be the kind of woman that makes him want to protect and provide for you. That's what draws him back." She held me in her arms and rocked me back and forth in her room.

Soon, Faith knocked on the door.

"Is Jim back?" I asked.

"No. I just wanted to know if you were all right."

"Yes. Have Cumby put Jeremy to bed," I said, wiping my eyes.

"Why don't you put him to bed, Rachel? He's your child."

"If I left the room, I would run from the house into town and get him back from Jerusha."

"Jeremy's already asleep," Faith said. "I'm leaving now, Mamma," she said.

It had been my doing. I went to the back porch and sat by myself for awhile. I was going after Jim when Bethanna went to bed. Jim had loved me and I chose Mamma instead. "Leave me alone," I said when Kileen and Pruddy came to the back porch to sit with me in the dark.

"Lord we're almost to the top of the hill," I heard Bethanna say when she turned off the light in the kitchen.

I cried in the dark and must have slept awhile on the back porch. I felt the bed move and woke suddenly. Someone was beside me.

"Jim."

"Yes."

It was him. I felt him in my arms. I kissed him and cried with relief. He sobbed once, his head on my chest. Then kissed me. I had waited for him and he was back. He had come back to me.

Fort Cobb, Louisiana

When Jim opened the door of our barracks at Fort Cobb, I had Jeremy in my arms. Cumby followed with a suitcase. I could smell the room before Jim opened the drapes. We had left Madill at four in the morning and had driven all day. The last of the sun was on the edge of the sky.

"You didn't take care of the place," I said.

He had given Jerusha a chance to come back for her things. When he turned on the lights, the ramshackle room gripped me.

"How could you—?" I walked into the bedroom and kitchen. Newspaper, clothes, plates with food still on them—trash everywhere. Empty bottles and cans sat on the table. The coffee pot was burned and Grandma's bowl was broken. The iron skillet rusted in greasy water.

I felt my rage at them. No doubt they had a good time. They didn't do anything but sleep together.

"Rachel," Jim started.

I shook my head. "Don't say anything." I didn't want him to talk to me. My throat tightened and tears came to my eyes. Cumby, not understanding the mess she saw, cried too. The door had been closed to Jeremy's small room, and it was the only room not touched by Jerusha. I threw the duffle bag with his christening gown into his room and told Cumby to rock him to sleep.

I was angry with Jim that he would bring me to such a place. Jerusha had slept with my husband, had hung her jeans in my closet, and I was supposed to accept it and clean up after her. I closed our bedroom door and sobbed against it. The covers of the bed were in a heap, the sheets dirty. Jim's fatigues were in a pile in the corner. Towels had been left damp on the floor. I could smell their filth.

"How could you leave the barracks like this?" I screamed when Jim tried to get in the door. "Bethanna never let things get in such a state—."

"Rachel," he said, "I didn't know it was this bad." He pushed the door open. "We've both been wrong. We've both hurt the other. We have to forgive one another." He tried to get me to look at him. I hit his hand away from my face and he took my head between his hands. "We've made love again, Rachel. I know you love me. Don't go back."

I couldn't look at him but only sobbed and pushed him away from me.

"Rachel, I'm sorry. I'll clean it up. Don't cry." I tried to leave the bedroom but he wouldn't let me. "You didn't take care of the barracks either when you were here," he reminded me. "I did the cleaning."

"I didn't let wet towels mold on the floor. I didn't leave the evidence of our lovemaking everywhere—."

"You leave me now, Rachel," he said, "and I won't come after you."

Cumby and Jeremy stood in the door of his room watching us. I turned to our bedroom and swallowed a lump in my throat. I yanked the covers and sheets from the bed and piled them with the dirty clothes in the corner.

"We'll sleep on the mattress until I can wash the sheets," I said spitefully. I went to the kitchen for a sack and returned to the bedroom. "Put the trash in here," I told him, "and get that pile of laundry."

He took the sack from me. "We'll clean it up together. Don't order me, Rachel," he said.

Jeremy started crying and I went to his room. Cumby and I got him ready for bed and put him in the crib. Cumby jostled his bed while I patted his back.

"I'm so tired, Cumby," I said presently. "I'm going to get him some milk. I don't have patience to stand here tonight."

I left the room. "Where's the sack with the milk in it?" I asked Jim.

We had stopped at the commissary before we came to the barracks. He went to the jeep to get it for me, then got the broom and returned to our bedroom. I opened the refrigerator to put the bottle of milk in but closed the door.

"There's spoiled food!" I yelled. "Didn't you take care of anything?" The smell nearly made me sick. There wasn't a corner of the barracks but Jeremy's room that they hadn't touched. "Didn't you ever do anything but screw?" I yelled when he came in the kitchen. I started to hit him, but he slapped me across the face.

"I can't do anything about it now, Rachel, but get it cleaned up. You left me and she came to take your place. Now shut up about it or I'll bring her back."

I tried to get away.

"I never knew you had a temper, Rachel."

"Nothing has ever made me so mad."

"You made me mad too. All those months in the hospital. You called for Bethanna. Bethanna. Beth-anna," he mocked me. "Never Jim. I was the one who was with you all the time but you never recognized me. You never called for me. Just your mother. But I'm here now, Rachel. It's Jim. And you'd better pay attention to me—. Now get Jeremy a bottle of milk so Cumby can get him to sleep."

I glared at him as I heard Jeremy scream from the other room.

"Do it now."

I took a bottle of milk to Cumby and she gave it to

Jeremy. Jim took my arm and led me to the bedroom. "Go to sleep, Rachel. We've got all day tomorrow to clean the place. I'll get Cumby a bed made on the couch."

I didn't want to go to sleep but Jim sat on the edge of the bed a moment until my tiredness made the room fade into highway passing beneath us—from Texas to the tall Louisiana pines and soon the road signs passed through the dark between the trees.

Runnels.

Waxahachie.

Dead Smith.

Scurry.

Upshur.

Uvalde.

Clegg.

It was Port Arthur once in Gulf saltwater that Kemp and Wallace cried. Wallace's father tried to pull him away but Bethanna wouldn't let go. It was the sting of red sky choking, and I woke suddenly and knew I was in the barracks. Jeremy cried in the other room. Jim slept beside me.

"I'll feed him, Cumby," I said. She woke too when she heard Jeremy. "You go back to the couch."

Jim had taken the spoiled food from the refrigerator and cleaned it. The only things on the shelves were the milk and the box of food we brought from Bethanna's, which Jim put in the refrigerator to keep the bugs from it.

I poured Jeremy's bottle of milk and took him from the crib. I went into the living room. Cumby pulled her legs up and I sat on the edge of the couch and fed Jeremy until I could wake up. Cumby's mouth twitched as I watched her fall back to sleep. The room was bare and plain. I closed my eyes until Jeremy finished the bottle and I put him in the highchair in the kitchen and fixed his cereal. By then I realized it was early in the morning.

"I have to go to the laundry," I said when Jim was awake. "I have to go to the commissary for soap and disinfectant. I threw the skillet and coffee pot away. We'll do without until you get paid," I said. "The dogs got into the trash you put at the backdoor and it is all over the yard." I asked Jim if he wanted oatmeal for breakfast that I had brought from Bethanna's. Jeremy and Cumby came to the laundromat with me.

The second night in the barracks, I was tired again. My suitcase fell from the bed when I opened it. The angels spilled out, confused for a moment as to where they were. Soon they flew around the room and then I didn't see them. I was going to sleep with Cumby in the living room because she wasn't used to sleeping by herself and she told me she cried in the night like Jeremy. But Jim told me I was going to sleep in the bed with him. I stayed with Cumby until she was asleep, then I got in bed with Jim. I thought he was asleep but he turned to me.

"It feels better with you here, Rachel," he said. "Forgive me."

"Aren't you going to love me, Jim?" I asked.

"We'll wait," he said.

For some reason, I wanted him to love me and still thought he would but I listened to him fall asleep and soon I slept also.

We have to have a base from which to start, I thought. Mine was going to be Fort Cobb, Louisiana. I had Jim and Jeremy and Cumby and the women and children in our barracks and quonsets around us. I was going to be a light in a dark place like Bethanna. I didn't have her anymore, nor any crayfish from Pole Cat Creek. Nothing would ever fill those places.

"Just look at those suckers," one of the women said as we sat on the steps of the barracks one afternoon. "Hey, bullet head, give that 'ere truck back."

"Little ass____." The mother got up and took the

toy from her child and gave it to the other one. The one who was now without the truck jumped up and down, screaming. He fell on the yard and pounded his feet into the ground. "Just look at the little f_____," his mother said.

The women laughed.

The base where Jim was stationed was a red little jelly bean, fat as the roly-polies Arthur used to keep in a jar. The field across from the base wavered. Yes, I nearly died, maybe I *had* died and they didn't tell me—and I was still living because I didn't know that I could have another chance to do what I should, and wouldn't go into the universe as shriveled as a crayfish. This was my chance. I was going to do it, *yes*; I was nearly to the top of the hill.

Cumby and I sat on the steps of the barracks in the afternoons and talked to the other women while the children played and fought around us. The tall pines pressed in upon Fort Cobb. They stood together like a wall, kept light from the ground. We went for a ride in the jeep and walked in the woods covered with a mat of pine needles. Jeremy tried to put them into his mouth and I yanked them from him.

Then Cumby wanted to go back to Bethanna in Madill. I said no she couldn't, not yet. It wasn't time. The road was still closed and she said it hadn't been and

I said yes, yes it had, and one night at supper she asked Jim and said I wouldn't let her go and he looked at me. The back of the chair somehow made the shadow of a wheel on the wall—a chariot wheel. The night would be all red. That little sucker.

Madill, Texas

When Jim got leave during winter maneuvers, we piled Cumby and her things into the jeep and started for Texas. She wanted Bethanna, just like I did. "Move over," I said, irritated with her in the small space of the jeep.

We stopped in Riler, Texas to see Jim's parents before Christmas. His mother looked at me with her dull eyes. I had been the one that caused Jim trouble. I hadn't been able to have a baby the way people usually did, and I made bills for Jim that he might never be able to pay.

I would work at the army base nursery when there was an opening, I told her. But she just looked at me. Jim's sister also looked at me with the same dull eyes. I liked Jim less when we were there. His parents faded into each other and their house was nearly as stark as the barracks. I thought I should appreciate Jim because he had more strength than his upbringing had given him. I had known Bethanna. Jim had no one like that.

Cumby upset his parents also. I heard Jim tell them she wasn't my sister, but an adopted child. The next day, I was glad to move on. We would be in Madill by afternoon.

Faith got married over Christmas. I stood beside her with Pruddy, Merrydean, Kileen and Cumby on my other side, remembering my own wedding in Madill Grace Church and the storm that followed into our marriage. I sighed. I would be like Bethanna with that faraway place in her eyes, seeing the other side of our troubles as though we were already past them.

"Faith, you married into a big family," I said as we came up the aisle after the ceremony. The church was crowded with people. We could hardly get through at the back. Arthur held a place open for us and we ducked under his arm. I stood beside Faith as she stood beside her husband.

They opened boxes and visited with everyone.

Mark was in mechanic school in Waco, Bethanna rejoiced to one of her friends. Wallace's father had taken him from us. Merrydean would be the next one married if she wasn't careful. The boys already crowded around her and she was still young, I thought.

I looked at Jim who talked to some of his old friends from Fort Jether. Cumby had Jeremy, walking with him through the crowd, spilling his cup on the shoes of the wedding guests. I should take him back to grandma's house. The crowd was closing in on me and I felt dizzy. Jeremy was tired and cranky. I looked at Jim another moment until he saw me watching him. I wondered if he wished he were one of the soldiers again without the burden of a wife and child. I pushed through the crowd of guests and Jim must have seen I wasn't feeling well because he took my arm and we left with Jeremy.

"The Lord's been good, he gave my husband back to me and my baby and we're at Fort Cobb and I'm going to stand for the Lord and be a wife and mother," I testified in Madill Grace Church on Sunday night before we left for Louisiana.

I knew we couldn't start over, but we were bound in events since the beginning, going on, having weddings and children for more weddings and children, gathering our mistakes and shortcomings like cotton in the field, being caught from the river before we saw the hook, cleaned, salted with pepper and spice, dried and smoked for the winter with molasses and bacon. And even when we were near death, it still seemed as if we walked, so that we used every minute to grow larger instead of smaller from our journey, and I leaned to Jim and asked him if I were dead and he said not to ask him that again. But instead of growing larger like we were supposed to, I knew we shrank like crayfish from the hardships of the journey, and the church that was built one board at a time with the labor of their hands, the sweat of their brows, was our meeting place, the Christian meeting place, because we were in America, Bethanna said, where the gospel was preached and we had the freedom to be the peculiar people that worshipped God and spoke with the Pentecostal stammer to the Texas dust when the red sun went down like a tomato on the prairie and the people could hear and laugh at us, and yet we prevailed in our days, the salt stain of our tears on the altar bench and the sweat from our foreheads as we tossed on the troubled sea of Texas and Louisiana and left our blood in the hospital beds in childbirth and our tears in the churches built with men's labor with the work of their hands because we had the freedom to labor for what we wanted and made the church because we wanted to worship.

And the woman was what a man worked for, wanted to work for and protect, because she was worth his labor and she was his love so that when they lay down at night she received the last force of his body from the day spent in labor, and the sweat of that labor was changed into the labor of love upon her and she received the seed that made the next generation to sit in the church that he made with his own hands and to worship the God that brought them out of the dust of

Texas and Louisiana and parted the waters and washed them in the blood of Christ, purchased them with the blood until he said, *here*, God, is your nickel. These folks are mine. Whosoever believes is drawn over the edge of the Earth into the red sun though he feels as if he's dead and just doesn't know it yet, suckered to live with Christ in the great wide universe we can't see as yet, but only inhabit so far by faith, and not a crony, no, he is a real God, a kind *Father*, a believable maker who changes us from crayfish to lobster. And that's the way it was in Madill, Texas, and Louisiana and Kansas and Oklahoma where we had lived, and probably in other places where I had not been, and maybe in other countries I would never know, being born in the wide continent of America that I would probably never leave.

I cried as Jim put my suitcase in the car and we left Bethanna and the family.

Maybe the angels got caught in my suitcase, I thought as we drove away.

"What were you thinking of at Faith's wedding reception in the hall when you looked at me?" Jim asked as we drove away.

I thought a minute. "I don't remember," I said when we were on the highway.

Some clouds crossed the sky as we left Madill. I hoped for a moment a sudden storm would hold us back from leaving. But it wouldn't. "Have you ever driven on ice before?"

"Not much," he said. "But I can do it without your help," he told me as I held Jeremy.

"There's nothing in Grandma's house," Bethanna had said before we left, "but what we carry with us." And I was obeying and paying the price, but where was the spirit Bethanna had? Maybe when I was pickled with the years like she was, salted and peppered and spiced and smoked, I would not dread the army base, but could walk like she did anywhere. Maybe I would be the piece of furniture in the barracks. Bethanna said it would come.

I waited.

"What were you thinking about?" Jim asked again.

"In the hall at the reception?"

"Yes."

"Why?" I asked.

"You had a look on your face I liked. I hadn't seen it in awhile."

"I was thinking of you," I said.

Jim reached over and tousled Jeremy's hair. He put his hand on my shoulder and looked at me a moment as he drove on the wet highway toward Louisiana.

Fort Cobb, Louisiana

I sat on the barracks steps pulling the strings of hair from across my face. The March wind roared and whistled, bullied whatever was not tied down.

I had washed clothes in a backyard tub and hung them on the line. They dried in half an hour, but for the jeans. It took them half a day. I pulled weeds along the barracks and along a row of vegetables I had planted in the coarse Louisiana soil, but they did not look like they would last.

"The f___ you won't." I heard a neighbor's voice.

After lunch, I put Jeremy in his crib and I slept too. When he woke, I put beans to soak in the crock, then I sat on the barracks steps in the wind.

I watched the children mothering Jeremy in the yard. I thought petunias might grow along the walk, but decided they would only be trampled. Jeremy picked up a stick and put it in his mouth as he toddled. The girls took it from him and his legs went limp, crying, angry at the girls who wouldn't leave him alone; he kicked his feet on the walk.

I hummed like Bethanna had done when I sat

beside her in the afternoons. Only now I hoped the afternoon would pass.

"Would you like to hear about Jesus?" I asked the children. The wind whipped the clouds above the barracks like they were eggs and there was a clamoring noise of distant artillery fire. Jeremy stood behind me on the next step, with his arm around my neck so the girls wouldn't get him.

The children had ugly faces and they wore clothes that should have been in the ragbag last summer. I had worked at the army base nursery awhile but soon quit because I didn't like the regimen they followed. I thought I could work with the children who ran loose in the yard of our barracks.

They scratched their arms. One looked at the other. "Who's he?"

I told them that Jesus was God's son who came to die for my sins.

"Why'd he do that?"

"Because God wanted me in heaven with him and I couldn't go because I was bad."

They looked at one another.

"Wha'd you do?"

"I did what I wanted to instead of what God wanted me to." I loosened Jeremy's arms from around my neck. He sat on my lap and when the girls reached for him he protested with a loud voice and jerked away from them.

"Leave him alone for awhile," I told them.

"What did he want you to do?" a child asked.

"He wanted me to accept Jesus as my Savior and then to obey him."

"I heard of him."

"I heard 'a im," another echoed.

"Who are you?" I asked the boy.

"Joel."

"Joel what?"

"Joel Stovalls."

"Well, Joel. Jesus was a man born a long time ago. He called some other men to go with him and they traveled all around the land preaching and healing the sick and lame. And when Jesus was nailed to the cross our sins died with him—if I accept Jesus as my Savior."

The children stood before me.

Lord, I thought. I'd heard it all my life. Why wasn't it easy to tell them. Joel Stovalls rubbed his head, shook his head as he thought about what I said. Beth-anna could tell it and all the children in her kitchen understood. S___, I heard myself think. Why was it all so painful and heavy? Why was it more than I could bear—this heavy cross I had to carry because Jesus up and went off to heaven and left me holding the bag here on this army base?

"My grandpa's lame," Joel said. "Yep, he is." Joel scratched his head again and looked toward the edge of the yard. "He's mean."

"What's the matter with him," I asked.

"He can't walk."

"Yes, that's what lame is," I said. "How did it happen?"

"I dunno. He stays in his chair all day and says come kill me, let me die."

"That's what he says?" I asked.

"Yes."

I sat at the table after a supper of rice and red beans with Jim. The neighbor kids looked in the back door. Jeremy squealed. I put him down and he walked to the back door and pounded his open hands against it.

"Jeremy!" Jim yelled. "You'll poke the screen out. Damn," he said. "Doesn't anything last around here?"

"Not with kids," I said. "If he doesn't poke it out, they'll poke it in from the other way."

"Why do you let these kids hang around here, Rachel?" he asked.

"They've got to have someplace to go."

A piece of the red dawn came in the window. I got up and washed my face. I fed Jeremy in the high chair.

Jim ate at the table. He looked down at his bowl of fried mush and never spoke. He ate that way at meals, never looking up unless I asked him for something, unless I asked about his maneuvers, his day, or told him about my day, or unless Jeremy spilled something and he'd yell at him. "Meals are for eating," he said. At Bethanna's house we talked and laughed. But I was not with Bethanna anymore. I felt a lump rise in my throat and swallowed it.

It was not yet light and Jim was gone. I had the day with Jeremy and the children in the yard. I still didn't have strength to last. Some of it would be spent with Jeremy in sleep with a note left on the door in large letters for the children not to knock.

What were these days for—other than cooking, making the beds, sweeping the floor and folding laundry? Where was the pleasure I had known? I wrote to Bethanna, but didn't tell her much. I left my feelings in myself. I would start being the furniture. But I couldn't I knew as I cried.

The children gathered before me again when I sat on the steps with Jeremy. I told them we would have Bible school. Few listened, the others scuffled, talked, fought over who would sit by Jeremy. I had a deaf child that yelled if he didn't get his way. He couldn't listen, but Joel Stovalls heard everything I said. The children were cruel to one another. They cursed. I quit in the middle of Jesus on the Sea of Galilee before the storm got started that he quieted.

I had too many children before me or too few. Nothing was as I planned. I had several that wanted to listen. But there were more who didn't. I put my hand on them and said, be silent.

They looked at me.

"*Silence!*" I screamed at them.

They stood gawking at me with their mouths open for a moment. "If you want to stay here on my walk, on *my* steps, you have to be quiet while I talk. And you can't fight."

"This place ain't yours."

"Yes, it is. My things are inside. This barracks is *mine*."

"No it ain't. We're just here. It's the army's."

"While I'm here it's mine! And if you want to stay on my steps you have to *shut up!*"

They squirmed. The deaf boy made a noise and Joel clamped his hand quickly over the boy's mouth.

"Now, would you like to accept Jesus Christ as your Savior?"

"No," they said.

"Well, you little turds, I have to go inside now. It's time for our lunch." I jerked Jeremy off the steps before he had a chance to protest and opened the door. The children scrambled to get out of my way.

I fixed us a peanut butter sandwich with tears running into the halves I cut for us.

I waited until another day for Jesus to calm the Sea of Galilee. "Would you like to belong to Jesus who can make the waves be still?" I asked when I finished the story.

They nodded their heads that they would.

One child, running in the yard, fell and cut his head. The blood stained the collar of his shirt. Their attention turned to him, running to his barracks, screaming. The mother would probably take him to the infirmary. The children said it would hurt to get it fixed.

"Have you accepted Jesus as your Savior?" I brought them back to our conversation on the steps.

"No," one of the boys said.

"Would you like to?"

Another boy grabbed his stick from him and he quickly turned to grab it back. I took it from the boy and handed it to its owner. He stood before me with a bruise under his eye.

"Do you understand Jesus took your sins and died on the cross?"

"I don't care."

"Would you say, come into my heart, Lord Jesus?"

"No."

"How can he come into your heart?" Joel asked. "It's all bloody in there?"

"Your heart means you—the part of you inside that thinks and feels and gets hurt and doesn't know what to do—." I turned my attention back to the boy. "Do you understand?"

He nodded his head that he did.

I looked straight at him. "Would you say, I have sinned and need your salvation." Tears leaked into the boy's eyes. I thought for a moment I should look away and not bother him, not bring him to tears, but I asked him again.

"Yes," he sobbed.

Let him cry, I thought. I kept talking to him about his salvation.

"I accept Christ as my Savior," he said in a small voice and I held him against my shoulder. He wiped his tears and snot on my blouse and I hugged him again. Let the army base fling its hardness at him, its cruel language, its poverty and abuse. The hopelessness. He would pass from it into the arms of the Lord who washed the deepest cesspool clean.

Mrs. Gustafson wanted me to bring the children to church when I told her about them. I knew the parents wouldn't mind. They appreciated anyone who would take the children off their hands for awhile, especially on a Sunday morning. But there was no way to get them there.

"One of the base buses—," I said to Jim.

"No."

"Could we at least take Jason and Joel Stovalls with us?" I asked. "There's room in the jeep for them," I said and he finally consented. "We need a van," I told him, but Jim said we couldn't afford one. "How can those people live the way they do? God doesn't like it. How can it appeal to them? They should be taking their children to church, but they stay out late on a Saturday night, get drunk, and can't get out of bed the next morning," I said. "If we had a van, Jim, we could take all the children to church with us."

"Can't you ever come in off the mission field?"

"Can't you ever really come home to me?"

Jim missed supper one night. He came in late, drunk. He stumbled toward me and I backed away from him.

"Rachel," he said and kissed me.

"I don't want you to love me," I said as he unbuttoned my nightshirt. "You're drunk."

He pulled me to the bed. I was his wife, he said. "I got you a van. I found a used one in the garage."

"Make love to me tomorrow, Jim, and tell me about the van then."

"No."

He was not going to change his mind and I was quiet until he finished.

"Are you the one been talking to the kids?" Frank Creagaree asked me as they tore down the van in the drive.

"Got to get Rachel on the road again," Jim said from under the van. He must have thought Franklin was talking to him and misunderstood what he said.

"You mean the Bible school on the steps?" I asked.

"Yes," he said.

"I've pretty much put off having it in the summer," I said. The children seemed bored with it anyway.

"And I thought I'd take her to New Orleans, except Rachel wouldn't want to go there. No, she only wants to go to her mamma's in Madill, Texas. Ain't that right, Rachel?"

"Yes."

"Jim's my friend and I don't want to cause trouble," Franklin said, "but neither do I want my kids becoming preachers," he told me quietly.

"Nor making you feel bad because you don't want to take them to Sunday school."

"Hand me the wrench, Creaker," Jim said and I walked away from him. "If Rachel doesn't feel the highway under her and see the road signs pass, she doesn't think she's living."

I sat on the steps in the evening with the sting of Franklin's rebuke while Jim banged on the engine under the van and Franklin directed him from above. The yard was full of kids, screaming, running, crying. They had running noses and scabs on their elbows and knees. Was there never anything but kids? How did Bethanna stand it? She never seemed to get tired of children.

There were some women talking in the next yard but they didn't pay any attention to me. The sky was reddish and I remembered the plum bushes in Madill as I sat on the steps watching Jeremy. The clouds grew as fidgety as Maclyn Howry. Jim sat up and wiped his face with an oily rag.

"Let's quit for now. It's nearly dark. There doesn't seem to be much use going on."

Franklin agreed.

The van was ten years old. It had ninety thousand miles on it. Franklin said that it had gone farther but the mileage was turned back.

"It needs another engine," Jim said. "But there isn't money for one."

Franklin wiped his hands on the rag and called his kids.

"Thanks, Creaker," Jim said as they left our yard.

Jim sat on the steps beside me and wiped the sweat from his face. He hadn't made love to me since the night he came home drunk. I put my hand on his neck and he looked at me. I kissed his dirty face.

"You smell like a car engine," I said.

"And sweat."

I smiled.

Arthur had enlisted at Fort Jether and was in line for a transfer to Fort Cobb. "Arthur can fix the van with you when he comes."

"I would rather have Mark," he said, but we didn't always know where he was since he finished mechanic's school.

"Could we really visit Bethanna sometime?"

"Yes, Rachel," Jim said. He was tired as we sat on the steps.

"Maybe we'll have some rain," I told him as we sat in the dark. "It would make my okra ripen." It was the only vegetable in the garden and it was nearly ready to pick. I had put a fence around it to keep the dogs and children out. "I'll make okra gumbo for you one of these days."

"I just get tired of not having any money," Jim said. "Dad gave me the money for the van."

"Wood?"

"No, Rachel. My father in Riler," he said. "I have parents too."

"I'm sorry, Jim," I said. "I didn't know he bought it for us."

"It didn't cost much," Jim said. "Now I know why. But I bought it that night I got drunk—." He left off what he was saying.

I put my hand on the back of his neck again and moved my fingers in his hair.

"Don't, Rachel. That gives me chills."

"I mean for it to, Jim. I'm going to put Jeremy to bed," I said and got up from the stairs.

"I can take care of children for pay," I said to Jim on Saturday when he went to work on the van again. "I'm stronger now."

He looked at me.

"We can use what I make for food, and Jeremy's shoes and a jacket for the fall." Jim was beating on a part of the motor with a hammer. "I can take the jeep to the country for berries. I'll make cattail and acorn flour like Bethanna does when she can't buy it at the store—and sumac and mulberry jam." I looked at him. "I know how to live off the land."

He looked at me again.

"We did it lots of times—but for a few things. We can use your pay for medical bills and another motor for the van."

Jim didn't say anything, but he continued to work on the engine.

"We can hunt and fish."

"I'll decide how we live, Rachel," he said, and banging on the motor once more, it split and fell to the ground, nearly missing his foot. He cursed and hit the side of the van with the hammer. Franklin Creagaree came to the drive and looked at the van with Jim. For once, I was glad to see him.

The barracks were uglier than I thought. I sat on the stairs while Jeremy played with a twig and the neighbors' children ran through the yards. Once he tried to follow them, but he got knocked down and Jim picked him up, howling, and returned him to me.

I squinted in the low sun across the army base as Jim and Franklin stood at the van. I thought I would make jambalaya and sweet potato pie if I could make anything I wanted to, and I thought how Jim would like that. But I wouldn't ask him for money. I knew he probably didn't have it and would feel bad telling me he didn't have even enough for sweet potato pie—or even tomato and apple salad. Anything sounded good. The base seemed to flare with red. And beyond the brilliant fire that encircled us was a terrible charred land. I put my hands to my eyes.

"Rachel," Jim took my shoulders. "Are you all right?"

"Yes," I answered.

"Don't scare me," he said.

"Everything seemed red for a moment."

Franklin was looking at me.

"Watch Jeremy," Jim said. "He'll run off again and get hurt."

"All right," I assured him.

A car passed on the street and honked, but I didn't pay any attention to it for a moment.

"There's no use in trying anything," Jim said. "We'll pull the rest of it out and look in the salvage yards for another motor."

Jim wiped his face again on the rag and stood with his hands on his hips. He and Creaker looked at the street when the small car that had passed, backed up with a knock in its engine. Even Jeremy turned to look at it. It stopped with a jerk at our drive and I heard a voice call, "Rachel!"

"Faith!" I walked to the curb. "Faith! What are you doing here?"

"We're going to Pole Cat Creek and we need a place to stay."

"Pole Cat Creek?"

"Wood is going to Louisiana until winter and Bethanna decided to come, even for the short while." We screamed and jumped together when she got out of the car.

"Are you living with her?"

"No. We're looking for a rent-house for her. Pat is between jobs. Bethanna hasn't felt good. The summer has been hot and dry in Texas. I thought we'd come ahead and get her a house so she can move into a place for once in her life without looking while they live out of the truck."

"She is all right?"

"Yes."

I spoke to Faith's husband. "We got a van," I told him. "And Jim's got the motor tore out of it. Not intentionally, but it fell out just as you drove up."

He looked at Jim. Faith clapped her hands at Jeremy and he came running to her.

"Know anything about cars?" Jim asked Faith's husband at the curb. They shook hands.

"Can't you tell by the sound of this one that I don't?" Pat said.

"We can just stay a day or so," Faith told Jim. "We're going to Pole Cat Creek. Your in-laws are moving back for awhile."

Jim looked at me. "That will make Rachel happy."

"Have you got room?" Faith asked Jim.

"Sure," Pat said, "we could have driven on to Pole Cat Creek in two hours, if we hadn't come out of our way to Fort Cobb—."

"I wanted to see Rachel—and Jeremy—." Faith jiggled him in her arms and he squealed.

Faith and I took Jeremy into the kitchen to talk while Jim and Creaker and Pat went to the salvage yard in Muleshoe.

"I harvested my garden, Faith," I said. "Got a few okra. Maybe next year it will be better. When Jim is a sergeant, we can live in Muleshoe."

"You look tired, Rachel."

"I would like to live off base," I said, half-ignoring her. "It's dirty here, not only the dust, but the people."

Faith held Jeremy on her lap.

"I don't have many friends. The women go to a bar in Muleshoe when their husbands are gone. I don't go with them and I guess I make them feel bad. It's hard to know what to do—."

"Wallace is back with us—Pruddy wants to stay with you when they first get back to Pole Cat Creek."

"I can't believe they're coming to Louisiana," I cried and we hugged each other again. "Bethanna doesn't write."

"I know," Faith said. "She doesn't have time."

"She really can't write either," I added. "Sometimes it takes me all day to figure out what she says."

"Are you fine?"

"Yes," I answered. "Are you sure you're not living with Bethanna?"

"No, we're not living with Bethanna," Faith assured me. "Are you sure you're all right?"

"Yes. I'm so damned hungry and tired of crud. Have you got any money, Faith?"

"A little."

"Let's make some jambalaya—we can see what I've got—go to the commissary and also make sweet potato pie for Jim and Pat. *Wheeoo!* I wish I'd paid more attention to the way Bethanna did things. If I knew how to make soap, I wouldn't have to buy it at the commissary. But I didn't pay attention when I was with her." I looked in my cabinets for what I had for the jambalaya.

Jeremy cried at the back door because he wanted outside, but Faith swung him to change his mind. He squealed in midair.

"I have bacon fat, tomatoes, pepper sauce and rice—and nothing for the sweet potato pie but flour."

"You have more than I thought you'd have. You sounded like your cupboards were empty."

"They are, nearly."

"There's someone at your back door," Faith said.

"I'm Carey Stovalls," the woman said. "I have to run an errand and need someone to stay with my father-in-law. I can't leave him alone. He's been too despondent." She looked at me a moment. "Jason said you'd do it."

"This is my sister, Faith Roark," I introduced them.

"I can't find my daughter. My husband is on bivouac. The boys are too young to handle him—."

"I'll come," I said. "Faith, you stay with Jeremy and count what I have in the penny jar. Give the angels our grocery list."

"I won't be gone long," Carey Stovalls apologized for bothering us and I followed her to their barracks.

When I went in, there was an old man in a wheelchair. The room whacked me with its meagerness. The sofa and chairs were battered. The walls scarred. There was an amateur radio operator's chart of the world on the wall—the patches of Europe, Africa, all out of proportion as though the world spun around the base in Louisiana elongating the farther away it got, like a game of crack the whip. Was that really the way the world was? No. I knew it wasn't. It only seemed that way in the Stovalls' barracks.

"Dad, Mrs. Satterethwait is going to stay with you while I'm gone."

He didn't respond but sat at the window as though he hadn't heard.

"I'm Rachel Satterethwait," I said, "and I'll stay until your daughter gets back."

He still didn't say anything until Carey left.

"She's my daughter-in-law," he said, "and I don't need anybody staying with me."

"I didn't have anything else to do and I wanted to come."

He must have recognized the lie in my voice. I couldn't speak for a moment. Something seemed to have a grip on the barracks. Hostility, I thought, or hopelessness. It was the opposite of what Bethanna's house was like. For a moment I wanted to run. I felt a panic rising in my throat. I sat at the window with him, looking out across the yard. "There's Joel, Mr. Stovalls," I said.

"Clyde Stovalls," he said.

"I wonder where Jason is—?" I looked at him a moment. "Oh, Clyde is your name." I hadn't understood him at first because I was afraid.

"Carey tells them to stay with me, but they don't. Everyone's always gone."

I tried to listen to him, but he smelled bad and some crusty skin on his nose made me feel sick.

"Jason and Joel would rather be out playing with their friends." His voice broke and he cried.

How could Carey Stovalls leave me with this man? I didn't know any of them except Joel and Jason. Clyde put his veined hand to his head and his body shook with sobs. I tried to comfort him. I didn't know what to do. I thought of screaming for Faith from the front door—Bethanna would know what to do.

"It's all right, Mr. Stovalls. I'm here with you. Carey will be back soon."

He hit me away from his arm. "She don't pay attention to me," he said. "None of them do—."

He looked at me with his sour eyes. "You could help me, little girl," he said. "You could bring me the razor blade they have on the top shelf of the cabinet where I can't reach. And you could cut across my arm here and then I won't be in the way no more." He had my arm in a tight grip and I tried to pull away from him. I jerked my arm once and his eyes riveted into mine. There was a light in his eyes then—a terrible, hurt glare. An evil I hadn't seen in anyone before. "Do unto others as they would have you do—," he said and I jerked away from him again with all my might and pulled him out of the chair. He hit his head on the window sill and fell to the floor. I screamed when I saw him on the floor, his crumpled legs folded under him, a bump rising already on his forehead.

"Oh!" I screamed. "I'm sorry. Mr. Stovalls. I didn't mean—." I ran to the door and called "Jason! Joel. *Joel!*"

Finally the boys came.

"I pulled your grandfather out of his chair by mistake. Help me get him back up."

Mr. Stovalls cried and slobbered on the floor. I looked at their panicked eyes when they saw how frightened I was. I didn't want Faith because she had Jeremy. Jim and Franklin were gone. "Get some man," I told them. "I don't care who. Just go to one of the doors and tell them I need someone in a hurry."

They ran back outside.

Mr. Stovalls gurgled on the foor and I looked at him. I wanted to bolt from the Stovalls's barracks but I couldn't leave him on the floor. I went to him and looked down. He panicked also. "You'll be all right. The boys are going for some help. I can't kill you. Why do you ask that? Don't *ever* say that to me again! No wonder they don't want to stay with you. I can't wait to get out either. I'll *never* come back!"

He reached out and hit my leg so quickly I fell to the floor beside him. He had his other arm over my neck with the power of a vice grip. I felt a scream swelter in my throat. The room turned red again—the worn chairs and sofa whirled about the room and elongated like Africa and Europe as they whirled. Something came out of them—it was spit and slobbers from Mr. Stovalls as he spattered his hatred at me.

I felt my arms and legs stretching out as far as the patchwork countries from the base on the map—my toe in southern Africa, whatever country was on its tip, a camel hump on the end of my foot. I laughed. Sudan. Port Arthur. No, that wasn't there. In Cape Town, pygmies dined at my ankle bone. I laughed to see them—. My fingers were in Germany, stirring the river like wash water for Jeremy's overalls and shirts stained red with berries. A burning pit stank. A steamer sank somewhere. Ribbons or streamers blew from some embassy—. Oh, it was bad. We didn't know. But the world went by like a giddy ride at a park and I was in a long line of people moving toward the edge and the world was red—all red, every bit of it, and we marched one by one to be gnarled by the pit over the edge and my turn was there so quickly. I tried to turn back but the movement of the great long line just pushed me ahead and as I fell below at the end of the long whirling line, a man with a hole in his jaw and teeth showing like a row of flowers at Grandma's house—and fingers scrawny as branches of the plum bushes in Madill—grabbed me and he was a horror to look at and I said to him this is not the way it is and he said yes it is. The camels looked up from their eating and I laughed, but I put the laughter back in my mouth because it wasn't time to laugh with us on the brink of the amateur's map swirling faster than we could stop. *Stop!* Let go. I would not be able to come back—and I still had something to do and I wondered how long this was taking—this life I couldn't remember exactly where it was at the moment because everything whirled and the man had me with his red hands. Jesus, I said. He held me tightly and though we were in outer space, he did not let go. And I felt the angels flap their arms again as if they had wings, and I said where have you been, I'm nearly dead in the grip of this looney man. But Jesus was the Savior and the angels were like His sweat when He worked. They were part of Jesus at the end of the world.

Just like in school I told him I remembered as a girl thinking we were riding on this globe that went fast through space, and I wondered why couldn't I see it with the road signs passing. As a child I thought of the Earth hurling through its orbit to get around the sun like Wood driving his truck when he had to be at work in another place with us slowing him down, taking all of his earnings. Why didn't he leave us and go on—. The angels stood there suddenly, a flock of them held me and the whirling Earth with love though it hit them again and again and splattered them with its slobbers—. They held on for dear life they gave the camels water and us their every breath because they had nothing else they were supposed to do.

"Rachel," Faith said gently. "Come on, Rachel. Wake up." But her voice was not gentle. It had something strange in it. I looked at her. My throat burned and I could not speak. Someone was there with something over my mouth again—There was a button in my throat after I had Jeremy. Did I have him yet? I tried to look but something held me down. I struggled to get away from it but it held me harder. I heard other noises—.

"He nearly strangled you to death, Rachel," Jim said. "What'd you go there for?" Jim paced the room. I saw the bare walls and knew I was in the army hospital again—.

"Let's go home," I said to him. "I can't stay here."

"You won't be here long, Rachel. Just for observation." Jim came to the bed and held me in his arms. "I can't lose you again, Rachel. That bastard nearly strangled you to death."

"Who?"

"Stovalls's father."

"Why'd he do it?"

"Distraught. They'll keep him in the hospital now."

I cried into Jim's arms.

"It's all right, Rachel. He won't do it again."

"He wanted me to kill him," I sobbed. "Can you imagine asking that?"

"I would have done it for him if I had been there."

"Don't say that, Jim."

He held me tightly against him for a while longer

and when he let me go I said, "Things are different than we see them. Will you remember that, Jim?" I wanted to tell him more but I couldn't think of what to say.

"Okay Rachel. You and your mamma's Christian love for the world—I know. I know."

Was it love or what was it Bethanna had for the world? Yes, love that understood something beyond the plainness of our lives—the want and hunger and never having enough, yet it was more than enough. And the artillery fire I could always hear just over the hill while I watched the planes that passed above the base one afternoon as I sat on the barracks steps with Jeremy and the angels and thought of how things were up there in space—the clouds elongated as we rushed by at such a pace—the horrid red man running with the earth as we ran toward the edge, his arms out like plum bushes and his eyes burning through our griefs.

I got up from the steps and walked to the Stovalls's barracks. No one was home. I walked back to our yard.

"What on earth are you doing, Rachel?" Faith said from the kitchen door.

"I have to talk to Carey Stovalls. But no one is there," I said to her. "Nothing happens too horrible for the man I saw when I was near death in their barracks. We can come to the end of this funny and terrible Earth and fall off its horrible edge and see what is there. Each step could do us in, Faith; our lives here are a vacuum as though we weren't even here. And there is something so strong holding us stronger than this earth and it pulls us against one another and we hurt each other and yet we both go on faster than we know, and whatever terrible thing is going to happen or already has—it cannot be more terrible than the man who holds us in the plum bushes of his hand—. Jesus went through hell to save us."

Faith sat on the steps with me.

"I have to tell that to Carey Stovalls," I said.

"I found a truck engine in the motor pool for the van," Jim said coming in one evening after Faith and Pat had gone. "I can get it next paycheck and they'll take the rest out of my checks over the next four months."

I looked at Jim. That meant I could visit Bethanna as soon as they moved to Pole Cat Creek. "Can you afford it?" I asked. "I think most of your paycheck goes for my old medical bills," I said. "I didn't think there was any left for anyone to take anything out of."

"It depends on you. Can you run the house on twenty-five dollars a week?"

"Yes," I said. "I've been wanting to take care of a few children soon."

"Just wait on that, Rachel. You wouldn't be able to travel to Bethanna's with a bunch of kids. Just wait—the time for that will come—," Jim told me. "You can babysit now and then, but not full time yet."

I kissed Jim with my hand to the back of his head. "I want you," I said. His hands were on me in places no one else had touched but him, would ever touch. "It's you, Jim," I said again. He was my husband. The man I longed for.

"Tell me again," he said.

"Jeremy's playing in his room."

"Rachel," he said when we closed the door of our room. He kissed my mouth and ear. "You made me wait for you," he said and kissed me again.

"Don't stop," I said. I felt his love and the heat of his passion for me as the hurt and disappointment and frustration of the day were forgotten with him.

Jim and Franklin Creagaree worked on the van for a week, pounding, soldering, cursing. There were not supposed to be any torn-down cars in the yards of the barracks, and the military police stopped and talked to Jim and Creaker one evening. They were in the middle of something and the policemen stayed until after dark, puzzling over the motor with them.

"It would be easier to make the van into an army truck to fit the engine," Creaker said.

Later Jim told me that one of the policemen was at the Stovalls's when Clyde tried to strangle me.

The Stovalls had been gone since the accident or whatever that afternoon should be called. But as I stood at the van with Jim and Creager one evening, I saw Carey drive up suddenly and go into the barracks. Jim had his head down at the motor and didn't see her, but Creaker did.

I put my hand to my mouth to tell him not to say anything.

I wanted to talk to her. I wanted to tell her I didn't have hard feelings against them. I started for her yard and heard Jim call after me. I knocked on her door before he reached me to try and persuade me to return to our yard.

"Mrs. Stovalls," I called. I knew she was inside and maybe wasn't going to answer the door. "I'm not angry at what happened."

"Rachel, come on," Jim pleaded. "You'll make it worse."

"We come to the end and think there's no way to go on but that isn't all that matters—. There's other things that count more than what goes on here. You don't have to stay away."

Jim pulled my arm. "Rachel—."

"This is your barracks. Bring Jason and Joel back. Let's go on—."

Jim had me nearly on our yard. "Why can't you just shut up, Rachel?"

I jerked my arm away from him. "When do I need you to tell me who I can talk to?"

"I filed charges against Clyde Stovalls."

"What?"

"I don't want him here where he can hurt anyone again."

"He didn't mean it, Jim."

"He did, Rachel. How can you be so stupid? You're going to take your Christian feelings out in the world and get tromped. You already have—"

I saw Carey's face at the window and told her there was someone who cared for us. I tried to indicate the sky and knew she didn't know what I meant. I saw her face crunched up like she was crying or screaming for me to go away.

"Rachel—."

"Leave me alone," I said. "I don't know how to tell her what I mean anyway. It doesn't make sense." I went into the barracks crying.

Arthur was transferred to Fort Cobb early in the fall. Pruddy and Arthur's girl came to stay with us until Bethanna got settled in Pole Cat Creek.

Arthur adjusted the truck motor to the van with Jim and Creaker, and we decided to take it to Tarpleys, fifty miles away in the Bayou Teche. If the van could make it that far and back, we could go anywhere, Jim told me.

On Friday night we got in our ten-year-old van and Jim cheered when the motor started.

"Yaw haw!" Arthur yelled from the window as we backed over the curb and Pruddy's soldier bumped his head on the roof of the van.

"I can't see out the back." Jim apologized for the jolt.

And no wonder, I thought. Jim and Arthur and Arthur's girl, and Jeremy, Pruddy, and a boy from the base, a newly-enlisted private named Ben, whom Arthur got for Pruddy, and I, were all in the small van. We also had our provisions and blankets and fishing poles for the weekend. Even the angels shoved us for more room.

We laughed as the van sputtered from the guard's station at the entrance of Fort Cobb and we turned south when we got to the highway.

We rode through the Louisiana country, past fields of oats and rye and the rows of cotton in fields.

Lafayette—.

The road signs passed and I hummed as Bethanna

had done. Jeremy was asleep on the private's lap beside Pruddy.

We stopped in a small town. I hadn't seen its name. My knees felt weak from the traveling and the strain of not yet trusting the van, I suppose.

It was like it was before when we traveled on the road all those years, and I was with Bethanna and the glory that was in heaven and only now and then shifted down to earth, shifted across the bayou and plains and took us upon it as though we were already resurrected from our graves. And it was as it had always been and why did not anyone else on the terrible army base see it? With all its stifling corners, did they never long for this?

Arthur gave a coyote call from the back window on the road and Jeremy, who had woken, looked at him.

"That's your crazy uncle," I said to Jeremy.

"Every family's got one," Pruddy said.

"He's ours."

We waved at the dirt farmers along the road. We were soon in Cajun country along the Bayou Teche. We passed stilted bridges that took the railroad over swamps. We passed the *pirogues*, manned on the water with push-poles. They were the only boats that could get through the web of humus and roots of the swamp muck.

We came to the ridge-settlements of Cajun

houses that sat on old cypress stumps and had painted fronts and doors that opened out to conserve space inside, and the stairs to the small attic room, the *grenier*, were on the outside too. And we saw the Cajun people, rural, Catholic, with names like Bujones, Horchow, Chenier, Domengeaux, crowded with their barefooted children into the small houses and speaking a French dialect.

"Tu comprends, non?" a man asked when we stopped for gas. I filled the water jug at the spigot.

"Non," Arthur said as Jim put gas in the tank and we drove on.

"How can we sleep on the road?" Cornella asked Arthur.

"There's enough of us," Arthur told his girl, "that we don't have to worry. Rachel and Pruddy are one of them anyway."

"We're not Cajuns."

"Close to it," Jim insisted.

"We'll put Ben on duty tonight," Arthur said.

St. Martinville.

Loreauville.

New Iberia.

I read the road signs as they passed with the slow rhythm of Bethanna's humming I remembered, and the wind coming in the window caught the hair at the back of my neck.

"I'm cold, Jim," I said. "I'm going to roll up the window."

"Where is Tarpleys?" Arthur's girl asked again.

"Just beyond Ruiz Landing," he said. "Not much farther."

A car came around the curve ahead of us too fast. Jim swerved and honked and Arthur yelled, *yahoo*, from the back window. Jeremy looked at him.

"Do you want to sit with your uncle?"

Jeremy nodded his head that he did and we passed him back to Arthur who made clown faces for him.

Jeremy laughed and clapped his hands in the air.

"I think you got a preacher there."

"Say on, brother," Pruddy said.

Jeremy clapped all the more at their encouragement.

We looked for a dirt road after we passed Ruiz Landing. Arthur pointed to it when he saw it and Jim turned off the highway.

"Cafful there, m'sieu," Arthur affected the Cajun talk to Jim who was driving too fast down the dirt road. *"Un fil est wet,"* Arthur handed Jeremy back to me.

We passed a cemetery by the river. "Wish this was All Saint's Eve when they walk with their candles from the church to the cemetery—."

"Mere, fils, bebe, oncle, tante, purrain," Arthur went on.

"Get the fishing poles," Ben said when Jim stopped. "I'm hungry."

"And the traps."

"Watch for the muskrat traps," I heard Arthur tell Ben as they left, "and them moss-pickers in the swamp trees."

I laughed and held Jeremy, who cried to go with them. We made a fire and camp while they were gone. I put a red cloth on the ground and lit the lantern. We had crayfish when they returned. The birds were so loud sometimes that we could hardly talk. I had chills in the swamp-damp night and held onto Jim's arm as we watched the fire. It was almost like it was at Pole Cat Creek with Bethanna under the moss-laden trees by the river.

"I feel like a parachutist in an armored tank division," Arthur said. *"Mon Dieu protek us."*

As long as there were places like Pole Cat Creek and Tarpleys I could get past the clunk I always felt when I returned to the base. I could lose the life I wanted and go on in that place that was washed of what I called life. There was more than just what was before our eyes, and I felt it seeping into me slowly as I listened to the angels snore—. A little chunk was first tasted through Bethanna in Madill, Texas, and it stretched into Louisiana where the crayfish grew big again.

COLOPHON

The text was set in Caslon, a typeface
designed by William Caslon I
(1692-1766). This face designed in
1725 has gone through many
incarnations. It was the mainstay of
British printers for over one hundred
years and remains very popular today.
The version used here is Adobe Caslon.
The display faces are Ensigna, Melior
and Mistral.

Composed by Alabama Book
Composition, Deatsville, Alabama.

The book was printed by
Thomson-Shore, Inc., Dexter, Michigan
on acid free paper.